"I wish I was working with you by choice and not circumstance. Not that I would choose to," Shanna said with a chuckle.

"If it weren't for this situation, we would still be throwing daggers at each other during leadership meetings," Lynx replied.

"I would have resigned if I didn't have a mother and sister to consider."

He got to his feet and went over to her. "You're right. I'm thinking like a single man. If I were married or had other responsibilities, I'd do what I'd have to and keep my job. I was hoping—" He stopped.

"No need to stop on my account."

"I'm ready to fall in love, get married and install the white picket fence. I'm at the brink of where I want to be professionally. I want someone to share my success with me."

"I get it," she whispered, tilting her head at an angle. A silent invitation for him to kiss her.

He had to oblige. He kissed her lips before using his tongue to lick her ear and behind her earlobe, loving the moan she produced. He placed tender kisses on her neck and cheeks before capturing her mouth. It was as hot and sweet as he remembered.

He could kiss her like this for hours.

Dear Reader,

Thank you for choosing *Rivals at Love Creek*. I am a big fan of small-town series romances and I am grateful for the chance to introduce you to the Harrington family. I can't wait for you to meet more of the Harrington men as they find love in the fictitious town of Love Creek, Florida. It was important to me that you meet a strong heroine like Shanna, who does her best to care for her family and those around her. However, though she is quite capable, it is wonderful that she will find a great support system in Lynx. I hope you will fall in love with this couple as I did.

Happy reading! I would love to hear from you. Please consider joining my mailing list at www.michellelindorice.com.

Best,

Michelle

Rivals at
Love Creek

—

MICHELLE LINDO-RICE

HARLEQUIN®
SPECIAL
EDITION™

Recycling programs
for this product may
not exist in your area.

ISBN-13: 978-1-335-72406-9

Rivals at Love Creek

Copyright © 2022 by Michelle Lindo-Rice

Harlequin Enterprises ULC
22 Adelaide St. West, 41st Floor
Toronto, Ontario M5H 4E3, Canada
www.Harlequin.com

Printed in U.S.A.

Michelle Lindo-Rice is a 2021 Emma Award winner and a 2021 Vivian Award finalist. Michelle enjoys reading and crafting fiction across genres. Originally from Jamaica, West Indies, she has earned degrees from New York University; SUNY at Stony Brook; Teachers College, Columbia University; and Argosy University; and has been an educator for over twenty years. She also writes as Zoey Marie Jackson.

Books by Michelle Lindo-Rice

Harlequin Special Edition

Seven Brides for Seven Brothers

Rivals at Love Creek

Visit the Author Profile page at Harlequin.com.

For my sisters and my sister-friends,
who stand by me: Colette, Glenda, Lea, Michele, Zara.

Thank you to Sobi Burbano and Fran Purnell,
who read my first drafts and give me timely feedback.
Thank you to my editor, Gail,
and my agent, Latoya, who helped me bring the
Seven Brides for Seven Brothers vision to life.

And as always, much love to John, Eric and Jordan.

Chapter One

All it took was one social media post for Shanna Jacobs's life to become entangled like a ball of twine. From a young age, she had learned to smile even when she was feeling broken inside. She had carried that lesson with her for her entire thirty-three years and became good at playing the part.

Seated across from Patrick Harrington in one of the black leather chairs in his office, she couldn't pretend the situation that had brought her here was nothing. She couldn't pretend it would pass like a Florida thunderstorm.

Not after the superintendent of the Love Creek school district's words: "I'm sorry, Shanna. This scandal might affect your consideration for the superintendent's position."

That meant Lynx Harrington—the principal of Love Creek High and her enemy, of sorts—would become the top candidate. Okay, since she had once fancied herself in love with Lynx when she was a teen, she couldn't call him her enemy.

Now he was her competition.

Serious competition.

Before Shanna could open her mouth to answer, Patrick continued with, "In fact, your job might be on the line."

Shanna gripped the chair, glad she was sitting, because her legs felt weak. Patrick's office boasted two conference rooms, a private bathroom and a large oak desk that had been handcrafted by one of his seven sons. Every time she entered this room, Shanna pictured herself occupying this space, her certificates and diploma on the wall, each of her plants tucked in the corners of the large room.

The past five days had ripped through her life with the savagery of a tornado after Austin Green, a twelfth grader who had graduated with honors, posted on social media that he'd had help on the SATs. From a teacher. Help that had led to his Columbia University acceptance.

"You would fire me?" she sputtered. "Patrick, you know me. You know I'm not involved in this mess."

"The board already terminated Todd and Mark," Patrick said, his tone somewhat accusatory.

"You made me hire them," she said. "They were your choices. Not mine." Patrick had wanted them because of their coaching background. He'd had plans for their football and basketball teams.

"I'm aware of that. But they were under your leadership. Your guidance. At least, that's how the board—the nation—sees it."

She leaned forward and jabbed a finger on the desk. "I can't be held responsible for the actions of two grown men who were all about winning. That's how we got into this predicament."

Austin had bragged in his series of tweets that Todd Smith and Mark Houghton, her assistant principals, had been behind the plan. Then he'd stated he wasn't the only one who had been provided with answers. His post had gone viral in hours, and the ensuing frenzy was one she would remember for a lifetime. Austin had already been interviewed, along with four other students from the graduating class.

Cheating.

On the SATs.

Three teachers had also been fired two days before Shanna had been summoned to Patrick's office. She was next. Just thinking about it made her stomach queasy, but Shanna was a fighter.

She pinned her boss with a glare. "Where do you stand? How do you see it?"

"It doesn't matter what I think."

"It does to me."

"I know you're not involved, but with everything going on, I think it might be best if you resign."

Resign. Give up. Her chin wobbled, and her eyes welled up. The fact that everything had happened under her watch was unacceptable. Like black ink splattered across a white page, this scandal was a huge slash through her impeccable record and stellar career. All she had done to overcome her broken past would be blotted out, tarnished because of other people's misdeeds.

"I'm not going anywhere," Shanna said, jumping to her feet. "Unless you plan to fire me, I'm going back to my office."

"I'm not firing you," he said after clearing his throat. "I was hoping you would—"

"Slink away like I'm guilty?" Eyeing a photo of Patrick with his son, Lynx, she lifted her chin. "Not a chance. Finish your investigation. I'm sure at the end of all this, I'll be vindicated." Then she would prepare for the most important interview of her career.

He got to his feet, ignoring that the suit jacket on the back of his chair had fallen to the ground. "I'm on your side, Shanna. I'm confident you'll be cleared, but your reputation is another matter."

"I'll be fine," she said, her heart pounding in her chest. "And when this is all over, I will put in for the superintendent position." After all these years of hard work, she wasn't about to let her prize go. The finish line was too close. And if she ran away, Lynx would win.

She wasn't having that.

Patrick shook his head and stuffed his hands into his pants pocket. "I think you're making a big mistake. I could give you a glowing recommendation, and you can move to another state and salvage your career."

"Love Creek is my home," she said, pointing her index finger downward. "I'm not going anywhere. No scandal is going to run me out of this town."

Patrick clamped his lips. "This isn't going to get better, Shanna. This scandal is like a sore that's growing and gathering pus."

She cocked her head and placed a hand on her hip. "I thought you, more than anyone, would be urging me to fight. Unless...you're using this to get me out of the way so your son can get the superintendent position. Because we both know I would've won." Shanna couldn't believe her sass, but she couldn't say she regretted her bitter words.

His eyes darkened, and his voice held steel. "Since you're under a lot of stress, I'm going to excuse what you just said. I have supported and mentored both you and Lynx—and quite frankly, I'm appalled that you would hint at any nepotism on my part. The school board conducts the interviews and determines my successor. You know that."

Properly chastised, Shanna squeaked out an apology before adding, "Within a week, this will be all over. You'll see." Her words lacked confidence, and her voice sounded shaky, which she hated.

"I'll be speaking with the board, and then I'll be in touch," Patrick said in a cool, dismissive tone.

All she could do was nod and hurry out of the room. She should not have mentioned Lynx, but it was hard to be around his father and not think of him. Especially since his photo was on display, boasting his lopsided grin, oozing with confidence, heating her blood to dangerous degrees.

Lynx had been the first man to take her heart, then smash it like crystal on concrete. A heart she had placed in his hands. A heart he had crushed because of a lie. If she could help it, Lynx wouldn't get the chance to get anything that should be hers.

And no scandal was going to keep that from happening.

She would be the next superintendent of Love Creek.

Chapter Two

A week after her meeting with Patrick, Shanna sat alone in her office at River's Edge High School and acknowledged the emotion coursing through her body.

Fear. Gut-shaking fear. Fear she could lose her job, her home, her career—and not because of anything of her own doing. Undeserved fear. Normally, her office centered, calmed her. She had chosen a shade of brown called Mexican Moonlight for her walls and had decorated the space with light oak furnishings, deep orange leather chairs, a loveseat and a large plush turquoise rug in the center of the room. She had a couple of plants, smooth jazz and a plug-in grapefruit-scented air freshener.

She scrolled through Austin's social media posts,

her heart racing in her chest like a bobcat chasing a squirrel as she read the responses.

A sob escaped, and the dam broke. Her shoulders shook under the weight of her tears.

Her mother needed health care.

Her sister, Yanique—"Yanni"—was in college, pursuing her master's degree in sociology.

Shanna lived modestly so she could support them. The thought of disappointing her mother and Yanni—or worse, no longer being able to support them—pierced her heart. She rested her head in her hands and gritted her teeth to keep from screaming before wiping her face. The worst part of this ordeal would be defending her ignorance. Ignorance of the plot happening under this very roof. Yet she would bear the blame like a halo. As the head of the school, anything that occurred within these walls ultimately rested on her shoulders.

Scooting her chair close to her desk, Shanna scanned more comments on social media before emitting a shocked gasp. The scandal had garnered national attention. People were coming for her from across the nation.

Despite her innocence.

This level of anxiety was overwhelming.

Shanna raced into the bathroom and upchucked her Caesar salad. Furious with herself for this act of weakness, she swished water in her mouth to rinse before washing her hands. Her cell pinged from on her desk. Shanna's cell and office phones had rung nonstop for days, but she had to make sure it wasn't her sister reaching out. She had received text messages from fellow administrators and Yanni. She had given all of them the same answer, which was that she was okay.

Shanna rushed to read the message on her phone and groaned. It was a text from Lynx, the last person she wanted to hear from. Never mind that her heart rate accelerated.

How can I help?

She read his words several times through narrowed eyes. Though her fingers shook, she wrote NONE NEEDED in all caps before hitting Send and dropping her phone onto the desk.

As if she would dare ask him for assistance. Not for one second would she believe the sender of that text meant those words. He was probably seeking a way to gloat at her downfall. He must have heard that she had once again been requested to meet with Patrick.

His response was a simple K. Like she wasn't worth the bother of an *O* before the *K*. Not that she cared. She just found it…interesting. With a shrug, she dismissed Lynx and returned to her spot on the chair.

Shanna decided to pull up her emails. Hundreds of well-wishers were reaching out. She rubbed her head and clicked out of her screen. No point in responding when she might be out of a job.

Another text came through.

Girl, I'm worried about you. Call me. Her heart lightened when she saw it was her best friend, Laurie Hightower. Since they both had iPhones, Shanna used FaceTime. She needed to see the face of someone who loved her. Laurie was about the same height as Shanna, except she had a deeper brown tone, to-die-for sharp cheekbones and a pair of sharp hazel eyes.

As soon as Laurie answered, more tears threatened.

"Girl, I know you told me not to call, but I can't get on that plane without talking to you." Her friend's eyes held a mixture of worry and sympathy. Laurie was on her way to Turks and Caicos to celebrate her engagement with her fiancé, Craig.

Shanna could see the bustle of the other passengers going by on the screen. "I don't want you worrying. I need you to celebrate for the both of us," she said, sniffling.

"I can't have a good time knowing my friend is in pain." Laurie chewed her bottom lip. "Maybe I shouldn't go."

"No. No. You must go. I can't be the reason why you have another broken engagement."

Laurie had been engaged four times, and each time, about a month before the wedding, she had ended things. She had earned the moniker the Runaway Beauty of Love Creek, a title Laurie hated with a passion.

"You know that's not even right," her friend said, tossing her hair. "You know I'm picky because of Cooper," she added, referencing her son and Shanna's godson.

"We're now boarding first-class passengers," Shanna heard the flight attendant call out.

"That's you." She blew a kiss. "Tell Craig I said hello, and please don't worry. Be safe."

Laurie looked ready to argue, but Craig ushered her off the phone after giving Shanna a quick wave. Shanna picked up her office phone and called the custodian to ask him if he could drive her car to the rear of the school. The news media was camped outside the building, waiting for her to emerge, and she hoped to thwart their plans.

Shanna powered off her cell and tossed it in her purse, shutting out all further communication. If only she could shut the scandal out of her life that easily.

Looking at the love seat tucked in the corner, where she had taken many naps before after-school games, and the walls lined with pictures of her with students and staff, Shanna tried to imagine vacating to make room for her replacement. She couldn't. Rubbing her eyes, she traipsed into her private bathroom and ran her fingers through her shoulder-length curls. She had dyed them a deep shade of brown with copper highlights, with a part down the middle. Next, she brushed her teeth and applied a plum lip color that enhanced her full lips and blended well with her chestnut skin tone.

Satisfied, Shanna gathered her belongings.

Lifting her chin, she forced herself to smile and stepped out of her office, closing the door behind her. She made sure to keep her eyes planted straight ahead as she trekked down the hallway, ignoring the curious looks of pity thrown her way. Thankfully, teachers and students were out on summer break, so she only encountered a handful of other twelve-month staff. Most of them had already departed to enjoy the Fourth of July holiday weekend.

The ten-foot blue-and-yellow cougar—the school mascot—at the end of the hallway that usually felt so welcoming now appeared sinister, its dark eyes jeering at her as she drew close. Shanna pulled her bag strap higher on her shoulder and nodded at the custodian, Carl Jenkins. He had served at River's Edge for over twenty years and knew all the comings and goings at the school better than Shanna did. It was close to four o'clock, an hour earlier than he usually came in, and she knew it was because of the scandal.

"I drove your Lincoln to the back lot like you asked, Miss Jacobs," Carl said, slipping the key into her palm.

"Thank you, Carl. I appreciate that so much."

She had purchased the Lincoln MKZ a month ago as an early birthday gift, but with her job on the line, she wasn't sure she would be able to make the payments. She had a nest egg, but it was reserved for emergencies.

"Anytime." He dabbed at his eyes. "I can't believe after all the positive things you've done, our school ended up making national news over this standardized-testing mess. This will all blow over. You'll see. I know you're a good person, and I know you wouldn't be a part of anything like this. I can reach out to the super and vouch for you, if you want."

She patted his wrinkled brown hand and said, "Thank you for your faith in me, but I don't want you reaching out or putting your name in the middle of this scandal."

He cleared his throat. "For what it's worth, I'm glad this school finally has a black female principal. It made me proud to see you up there at graduation time. You were the first, remember that, and no one can claim that but you."

Shanna gave a jerky nod. Whether Carl realized it or not, he was sort of telling her goodbye in his own way. His words deflated her optimism like a pin in a balloon. Her shoulders curved. She willed her feet to move and continued down the hallway toward the reception area, drawing deep breaths. *This doesn't have to be my final walk as principal in these halls*, she told herself.

Nancy Hughes, her secretary, sniffled and said, "I deactivated our Facebook and Twitter pages."

"I'm sorry this is happening," was all Shanna could say, swallowing. The guilt and burden of responsibility settled like bile in her stomach.

"I'll take care of your plants," Nancy choked out, covering her mouth with her hand.

Another goodbye.

"I watered them this morning," she managed to whisper.

Her first day on the job, she had carried in several potted and hanging plants: a ribbon plant, a philodendron, a corn plant and a Madagascar dragon tree. Then she'd placed one in each of the four corners of the outer office. She'd taken meticulous care of the plants, pruning them, ensuring they had the right amount of water, and they had flourished under her care. The lush greenery spilled out of their pots, healthy and vibrant, a physical reflection of her thriving career.

Despite her fragile situation, Shanna smiled.

Her mother would have been proud. When Bernice Jacobs had been diagnosed with early-onset dementia, it snatched away everything except for her love of plants. Shanna had bonded with her mother by learning all she could about the different kinds of plants. Luckily, she had inherited her mother's green thumb.

"You'll get it all sorted out. I hope I'll see you tomorrow." Nancy made the sign of the cross. Even as she spoke the words, Shanna could hear the uncertainty mixed with hope in Nancy's voice.

Shanna averted her gaze from the older woman's face. If she made eye contact, she knew she would break down, and she was determined to remain composed. She curled her fingers around the strap on her purse and squeezed. No eloquent parting words could be uttered, her throat tight under the strain of keeping it together.

She gave a small wave and pushed open the glass door to exit the administration office. The sunshine state's muggy, dry heat stifled her, stealing her breath as soon as she entered the main lobby of the school near the front entrance. The AC had been turned off in the rest of the two-story building to conserve energy, making it feel three times hotter than a steam room.

Keeping her back toward the front of the building, Shanna scurried toward another exit leading to the football field. The entire ten minutes it took to get to the rear of the massive building, all she could hear was the sound of her heels clicking to the tune of *Scan-dal, scan-dal*, echoing down the darkened hallway. This was when her tears flowed.

Once she was at the exit, Shanna placed a hand on the glass door and froze. Tears ran down her cheeks and down her chin. After all her wonderful days, she had to slink away and hide from the press. "This is not goodbye," she vowed and squared her shoulders. It couldn't be.

Drawing a deep breath, Shanna wiped her face with the back of her hand, clamped her jaw and pushed open the door. She peered outside and looked around with the stealth of a child stealing an ice-cream bar late at night before heaving a sigh of relief. An empty, open land of freshly mowed green grass awaited her.

Smoothing her dress, Shanna slapped on her sunglasses and treaded carefully across the field to ensure her three-inch pumps didn't sink deep into the grass. At five-nine, if she fell, she would land hard, and it wouldn't be pretty. It had stormed that morning before the sun came out, and the earth hadn't fully dried. Her heels dug into the wet ground, causing tiny drops of mud to hit her ankles.

Sweat beads rolled down her back. The sun's rays were merciless.

She wiped her brow, wishing she had thought to carry a bottle of water from the mini refrigerator in her office. Thank goodness she kept napkins and deodorant in her glove box, because she was surely going to need them.

Entering her vehicle, Shanna's shoulders slumped from relief. She hadn't been discovered. She pressed the start button, before applying deodorant and rubbing hand sanitizer on her hands. The vehicle gave a quiet hum, and the AC kicked on.

The clock read 4:12 p.m. She had about forty minutes before her appointment to pull herself together. She lifted the visor and looked into the mirror. Her face looked flushed, and she could see the worry in her eyes. "Don't fall apart," she told herself, even as her stomach constricted. The gravity of the situation barreled through her mind at full force.

For a quick second, Shanna debated skipping the meeting and jumping on the highway. But this was her life. There was no escaping it, and her mother hadn't taught her to skulk from the truth. She straightened and patted her curls. She wouldn't slink away in shame when she had done nothing wrong. Even if the nation believed otherwise, she knew the truth. She would stand on that. If today was to be her last day, she would leave with the glory of a comet trailing across the sky.

After her pep talk, Shanna retrieved the napkins to wipe her face and reapplied face powder; then she placed the car in gear.

Chapter Three

Lynx Harrington pulled the golf cart into the spot designated for the principal of Love Creek High School. He had spent most of the day helping his coach unload the new equipment for the second gymnasium that had finally finished being built. The Florida sun in the summer was brutal, and some of the members of the Navy ROTC and football team had passed out during practices a few days ago due to dehydration. Lynx had attended this very high school, and because of his size and bulk, he had been quarterback for the Love Creek Gators, so he knew about the danger of the sun.

He couldn't risk anyone suffering a heat stroke, so on days when the temperature was above ninety-five degrees, the gym would be a smarter, safer option.

Lynx had taken three years to fundraise, irritating businessmen in the area until he had the funds to break ground on the gym. Next up would be a new state-of-the-art theater. That's what he wanted to spend his summer working on—not talking about a scandal that had nothing to do with him. News media from across the country had been calling and emailing to get a statement. Of course, he hadn't complied. He heard they had set up a tent in the River's Edge parking lot. That's why he had reached out to Shanna, though he knew she would rebuff his help.

Still, he had tried.

And he had received a swift no.

It was close to 4:30 p.m., and all the other staff had left for the day. Dressed in the school colors—a burgundy polo imprinted with the words Love Creek High, along with a small replica of a gator, and a pair of tan slacks—Lynx had been overdressed for the Florida sun. He wished he could go home, stand under the shower and allow the heat to beat his sore muscles. Then he would work on his watches.

When he wasn't working for the school, Lynx focused on fixing his antique watches. When Patrick and Tanya Harrington adopted him, he had inherited a grandfather, Sterling "Pop" Harrington, who loved to repair old watches. Lynx had been drawn to the large, silent man, who looked like a brown version of Santa Claus, and he'd begged Pop to teach him. Together, they spent hours fixing all kinds of watches. When Pop died, Lynx had carried on his legacy. To date, he had fixed twenty watches and had sold some to other collectors.

Tinkering with his collection would have been an ideal end to the day. Instead, his father had called, requesting Lynx's presence at the district office. He called the custodian using his walkie-talkie and asked him to cover the golf cart and park it in the shed. He wasn't worried about the cart being stolen. With the school's name emblazoned on the side, it would be easy to find. Besides, Love Creek had been voted one of the best places to live because of its low crime rate. But he was concerned about the rain and bugs and snakes. When he navigated the school campus, Lynx didn't want unexpected traveling companions.

Lynx went into the building to use the restroom and wash his face and hands. He welcomed the cool air after being in the stifling heat for most of the day. He kept spares of the school shirts in his office. When he entered the office, he realized he had left on the television mounted opposite his desk. The volume was off, but the closed-captioning was on. After changing into a fresh polo, Lynx drank two bottles of water, reading the captions on the news channel.

Just as he took the last gulp, his cell phone rang.

Excitement rose when he saw the name on his screen. "Please tell me you have good news for me," Lynx said by way of greeting the older man on the phone. Pietro would only be calling for one reason.

"I have more than good news," Pietro said, Russian

accent thick. "I think I have found the watch you've been looking for. It fits the description to a tee."

Lynx's heart raced. "You're about to get my hopes up."

"It looks just like the one in the picture. I'm pretty sure that you finally made bingo. It's going to be in North Carolina this weekend."

Instinctively, Lynx felt his pocket for his wallet. "I was coming up that way, so I'll hit the auction house before I come back home. Text me the location. You best believe I'll be there. Thank you for looking out." Pop had given Lynx a picture of a special watch he'd had as a youth, and Lynx kept it in his wallet. The watch was considered an heirloom, dating back to the early nineteenth century. Pop had sold it to save his home and to support his family. Lynx had scoured garage sales and traveled across states to find it, but to no avail. He had to see if Pop's watch had been recovered.

"It's my pleasure," Pietro said.

Lynx pressed the button to start his Audi from inside his office. He couldn't wait to drive to North Carolina to investigate. If he hadn't made other plans, he would have already been on the highway. "Let me know how much I owe you for all this digging."

"Don't sweat it. You repaired my grandmother's watch when no one else would touch that smashed glass. So I'm glad to return the favor. I only wish I could be there to see your face when you get that timepiece in your hand."

"Man, it's going to take a lot to keep me from acting the fool."

The men wrapped up their conversation. A picture of the Love Creek district office flashed across the television screen. The brick building had once been the location of the town's first high school, with a total student population of 125 students. Then, once the town grew, the high school was relocated and the building repurposed. Five years ago, the building had been destroyed by a hurricane, and the school board had approved the two-story structure built out of brick and cement.

Lynx rushed to turn up the sound on the television. A reporter was rehashing the scandal, but his eyes were drawn to the woman threading her way through the mob to get inside.

Shanna.

She walked with poise and confidence, lifting a hand to ward off the questions. She looked close to six feet tall in those heels. The press followed her like she was the Pied Piper.

He quirked his lips, admitting that admiration swirled within. If he was the one facing the heat of speculation, he didn't know if he could keep his cool. Maybe Shanna was okay, he told himself as he exited the building and drove the half-mile distance to the Love Creek district office.

When Lynx swerved into the parking lot, his brows rose at the large number of reporters. It hadn't looked like so many on the television screen. Judging from the tents that lined the parking lot, it looked as if they had been there for hours.

Lynx understood why they were here, but he didn't like it. He searched for his sunglasses—a poor disguise, but they would cover his eyes. He slung his backpack on his shoulder before getting out of the car.

He would rather face twenty linebackers than the crowd of reporters. Glancing at his G-Shock, he saw he had ten minutes till he was scheduled to meet with his father. He sped up. His father and superintendent, Patrick Harrington, didn't tolerate tardiness.

Within seconds, Lynx found himself surrounded by microphones pushed close to his face. He lifted a hand to shield his eyes from the bright light of the cameras and stormed through the throng. He jutted his jaw, refusing to answer any questions tossed at him.

"Are you worried about your school coming under investigation?"

"What will happen to Ms. Jacobs?"

"Have you read the accusation on social media?"

Lynx kept moving, relieved when the crowd parted, though they followed him to the entrance. There was a sign on the door banning the press from entering the building. Since it was after-hours, he had to use his fob for access. Plodding past the reception desk and waiting area, Lynx arrived at another set of closed doors. These had been installed after a robbery at the local bank. He swiped the fob and took take the stairs to the second floor. He strode pass the Curriculum and Special Education departments before arriving at the superintendent suite, which boasted two conference rooms, a secretary's office and his father's office.

Lynx glanced into the smaller conference room, noting Shanna was in there with her back turned, then proceeded toward his father's office. He could hear the muffled sounds of his father's deep bass voice joined by another. His brother Caleb was present, which was no surprise, as Caleb was the school district's attorney. He rapped on the half-open door before entering.

His father and brother were huddled together, reading a document. As they stood side by side, with their jackets tossed onto the backs of their chairs and their shirtsleeves rolled up, the resemblance between them was strong. Both were the same height, with a lean build and pecan-toned skin, though Patrick sported a low fade and Caleb had a clean-shaven head. It was at these odd moments that Lynx remembered he was adopted. Patrick and Tanya Harrington had opened their hearts and home to foster two white brothers, and their lives had changed drastically.

For the better.

He would never stop thanking God.

Abandoned by their mother at five and seven, Lynx and his older brother, Hawk, had been welcomed into the Harrington household, which already had three boys—Tanya's son, Axel; and Patrick's sons, Drake and Ethan. Though Lynx and Hawk had jet-black hair and blue eyes, they blended in, their personalities meshing with the other boys. Soon after that, Patrick and Tanya welcomed fraternal twins, Brigg and Caleb. As the eldest of the now seven brothers, Hawk had claimed Brigg as his baby, and Lynx had claimed Caleb. All of them had grown to become "successful, contributing citizens to their country," To quote his father's words.

Lynx eyed the small platter of turkey sandwiches, potato chips and water bottles. He hadn't eaten since breakfast, and his stomach was quick to remind him.

Patrick waved a hand. "Susan's preparing a press statement to handle this mess. I have a few months left before I retire, and I don't want to go out with this mark on my record. I'd like you to look over it once I'm done."

Susan Phillips was the district press secretary and publicist.

Lynx dumped his backpack in the chair and pointed behind him. "I think I saw Shanna in the conference room?"

Shanna Jacobs.

Back then—his first crush.

Right now—his rival.

Since they'd met in third grade, Lynx and Shanna had been in competition, each desiring to do better than the other, a race that culminated with Shanna becoming valedictorian and Lynx salutatorian of Love Creek High. Some would say he was salty and a sore loser. But it was more than that.

He knew it.

She knew it.

"Yes, I set up a meeting with her. Caleb and I plan to talk with her, and we were hoping you'd join us."

"I'm not an HR person, so why would you want me here? Besides, given the choice, I don't think Shanna would want me involved," Lynx said. His entire family knew how he felt about Shanna Jacobs.

"It's not up to her," Patrick replied with steel in his tone. "My HR manager is on vacation, so this ordeal rests on my shoulders."

"Our social media page is filled with people clamoring for her to be replaced. With actresses like Felicity Huffman and Lori Loughlin making headlines for SAT bribery, this is something we can't sweep under the rug or ignore," Caleb said, rubbing his eyes. His brother spent too much time in the books and behind a computer screen. He was the only one of the seven brothers to need prescription lenses. Caleb had been in glasses since the fifth grade, before changing to contacts his freshman year at college.

Lynx made a mental note to invite his brother to go fishing or hiking—something, anything, to give Caleb a break from the books.

He snatched one of the turkey sandwiches off the tray and took a bite before continuing. "But Shanna isn't a celebrity. She's one of ours—Love Creek born and raised. Is that what we do to one of our own?"

Neither man answered.

Lynx stuffed another sandwich in his mouth and focused on the photos of his father's numerous awards and pictures that lined the rear wall. He strutted over to look at the one in the middle of Lynx accepting his principalship. He had graduated from the University of South Florida, top of his class, after earning both his bachelor's in education and master's degree in education administration. Patrick Harrington was the reason Lynx had chosen a career in education. He wanted to help other young men and women find their path, and he had done that.

Next to his picture was a photo of a young woman with full ruby-colored lips—lips he knew from experience were luscious and soft—smooth flawless skin and cinnamon-colored curls. Shanna had been beautiful as a teen, and she had aged like fine wine. She wore a bright smile, clutching her principalship certificate. Lynx knew Shanna had her eye on the superintendent position. She wanted it almost as much as he did.

His father came up behind him and tapped him on the shoulder.

Lynx shook himself to the present to focus on his father's words.

"I'd like to propose that you assume leadership at both schools. Then Shanna can remain in her position as your assistant. She will continue with her duties overseeing the hiring, training, discipline for all staff but will report to you."

Lynx's eyes went wide, and he swung around to look at his father. "You can't be serious? I won't agree to this." He splayed his hands. "There's no way she would go for that. I know I wouldn't."

Patrick folded his arms. "This is her only choice. The board wanted me to offer a termination package."

Termination.

For some reason, he couldn't bear the thought of that happening to her. He knew there was only one thing to do.

Chapter Four

Hope for the best.

Prepare for the worst.

She recited that mantra under her breath as the huge clock on the wall ticked. She was seated in the small conference room outside the superintendent's office.

The room smelled of new carpet and fresh paint. The walls were ecru-colored, and there was a huge picture of a tidal wave and another of the superintendent with other Florida superintendents, taken at a retreat. The men had been golfing, and Patrick Harrington had won the trophy, taking first prize.

Shanna squeezed her legs tight and clasped her shaky hands. She released small breaths and prayed every prayer she remembered from children's church.

Shanna eyed the oblong cherry table with high-back black leather chairs that seated up to ten, and jumped to her feet, heading over to the hanging grape ivy and Song of India plants.

They needed to be repotted and watered. She plucked a couple of dead leaves before tossing them into the garbage. All this to cover her nervousness and keep from barging into Patrick's office and demanding to know if she still had a job.

She stopped her pacing and made herself sit and wait.

Wait…while the two men in the other room decided her fate.

The way she saw it, the fact that they were making her wait wasn't a good sign.

Shanna had left her purse in her car along with her cell phone and now regretted that decision. Her thoughts became her company.

What if she was let go? Or maybe she would be transferred.

A better option, though not the one she preferred. Either way, Shanna needed to rehearse what she planned to say. She would be objective, matter-of-fact, while arguing her case.

When the door to Patrick's office opened sixteen minutes after she'd arrived, her mouth went dry at the sight of the three men coming out. The fact that they were related would scream nepotism if she didn't already know that each had achieved their positions through hard work and by being the top candidate during their interviews. Their relationship was also very indicative of how small Love Creek was, with the town boasting a population of 15,000.

Shanna straightened. She had no idea that Lynx was present. Maybe he had come to gloat over her demise in person. She kept her eyes pinned to Patrick to keep from shooting daggers Lynx's way. Every time they were in each other's presence, the tension thickened. She'd always found his dark hair, cerulean blue eyes and square jaw attractive, though she often avoided making eye contact.

Every time she saw him, her lips burned at the memory of their sweet, single kiss seventeen years ago. The question as to *why* she remembered lingered in the back of her mind. She smoothed out any creases in her dress.

Patrick settled at the head of the table. Lynx sat across from her, while Caleb sat beside her.

"Thank you, Shanna, for waiting," Patrick said with a practiced smile. "I have Caleb and Lynx with me because our directors of human resources and operations are on vacation. As we speak, Susan Phillips is working on our press release. I will be holding a press conference at six p.m. today. During that time, I plan to announce that Lynx will take temporary leadership of both high schools, with you serving as his assistant."

Assistant?

Her mouth hung open, and words deserted her. She looked at each of the men before her. Lynx pierced her with an icy stare, as if challenging her to say something.

She shook her head.

Still in processing mode.

Caleb placed a sheet of paper bearing the district's official logo in front of her and used his index finger to point to the signature line. "Take a moment and read through the memo. You'll need to sign there. Your signature does not indicate an agreement." His tone held sympathy, and her pride dove in to loosen her vocal cords.

"So this is it?" she hurled at the superintendent. "I thought you brought me here to have a discussion, to hear my side. I've been a loyal employee, spent my entire career here in Love Creek, and with the swoop of a pen, you're demoting me because of allegations?"

"Times have changed. Because of this incident, our school district is under intense scrutiny. We are under attack on social media, and the entire nation has its eye on us. I believe this is a reasonable solution."

"It isn't. Not for me," she said. "Making me work under Lynx means you've tried and convicted me without a proper interrogation."

"Shanna, that's enough," Patrick said.

Lynx was too busy inspecting his fingernails to add to the conversation.

"I disagree. This is not enough. I didn't do it." She drew a deep breath. "I'm many things, but a cheater isn't one of them."

Lynx's head shot up. His mocking expression grated her but this wasn't the time to confront him.

Caleb placed another letter before her. "We have written a letter of recommendation if you would prefer to seek another job in another town."

She shoved the recommendation back into Caleb's hands. "Oh, please. You and I know that no one will hire me. This is one of the drawbacks of living in a small town. If I leave, it would be seen as a sign of my culpability."

"I admire your grit and spunk," Patrick said. "That's one of the reasons I hired you to turn River's Edge around."

She leaned forward ignoring the sweat beads across her forehead. "Which is why demoting me will do more harm than good. I have put some wonderful initiatives in place—I believe this is the year we will see the benefits of the mentoring program and the behavior plan. I should be there at the helm to see it happen. I *earned* the principalship. Don't take it away from me."

She finally addressed the man across from her. "Did you know about this?" Her left eye ticked. "Is this your way of helping?"

"Not until twenty minutes ago. And, no, this isn't what I had in mind when I asked if you needed help."

"So I'm being demoted to appease the masses," Shanna said in a dull tone. Her heart ached at the insult, though she knew it was a generous offer considering her school was embroiled in a terrible scandal.

"You'd get to keep your job and your salary," Caleb said matter-of-factly.

She had always admired the younger Harrington's

poise and manners, but now his sensible demeanor appeared cold. She bit her tongue to keep from lashing out at him. He had the look of someone who thought they were helping.

"It's only temporary," Patrick offered. "A few weeks. Maybe a month or two, tops. Until we clear you of any involvement. Think of it as a sort of mentorship."

Susan Phillips popped inside, flashing papers in her hand. "I have both statements ready for your approval. Do you know which one you'll read?"

The clock on the wall registered 5:43 p.m.

Shanna's heart thumped. One paper held her demotion and the other, her termination. She wiped her brow., her curls damp on her face.

"Not yet." Patrick shot to his feet and beckoned to Susan and Caleb. "Let's give Shanna a moment to decide." He pointed to the clock. "You have five minutes."

Shanna gasped.

Five minutes to make a career-impacting decision. To eat crow.

The three other occupants departed, leaving Lynx alone with her. He rushed over to her side and tugged her to her feet.

"Can you do this?" he asked, chest heaving.

The room closed in around her. She felt like she could hardly breathe under the intensity of his stare. The blues of his eyes appeared deeper, and she wanted to touch the cowlick across his forehead. Shanna stepped back to put distance between them and to regain her equilibrium. All of a sudden, she was fighting two battles.

"Well? Can you?" Lynx demanded, walking back into her personal space.

They engaged in a weird tango until she found herself backed against a corner. Like a deer facing off with a mountain lion—that's how she felt.

"If it were anybody but you, I wouldn't hesitate." Shanna regretted her words as soon as they left her mouth. But she tossed her hair and met his gaze square on.

Lynx backed away as if he'd been scorched. "Well, it looks like I'm the only choice you've got. So what will it be?"

Her mother's and sister's faces flashed before her. Shanna knew she had to put their welfare above her own. She gave a nod.

"I need to hear you say the words," Lynx insisted.

She breathed out. "I'll work under you."

The innuendo of her statement appeared to hit them both at the same time. His mouth parted, and for a brief moment, there was a hint of desire in his eyes. She felt relief that she wasn't the only one experiencing a sudden heat.

"I meant I will work for you…" She paused. "Temporarily."

"Good," he ground out. "Just promise me you'll be honest with me. No underhanded stuff. I need you to clear all your decisions with me. Follow what I say, no questions asked. Understood?"

Shanna shoved past him to grab her keys off the

table. "I knew you would bring up the past. You just can't resist, can you? It was fifteen years ago. I wish you'd get over it. Whatever happened then, I've put it behind me." Well, not everything. But she wasn't going to humor that train of thought. "Why can't you do the same?" she asked, hating her pleading tone.

Lynx stepped in her way and folded his arms. He spoke in a low, commanding voice. "Answer me."

Her anger dissipated. She had no other option if she wanted to salvage her reputation. "Yes, I will do what you say." She hated how subservient she sounded, though she knew she had no intention of being accommodating.

Patrick returned, interrupting them. She watched the older man take in their proximity and moved to the other side of the room. "Have you made your decision?" he asked.

"Yes," she said, keeping her eyes locked on Lynx. "I'll do it."

"Good. That's all settled. Caleb will have the documents for you to sign," he said before clearing his throat. "There's something else you need to know. I'll be announcing my retirement in the fall as well at the press conference. I think that will be a good distraction from this situation."

Shanna shook her head and released short breaths. "The timing… I won't have a chance. You know that I wanted this."

"I know, and I am empathetic with your situation, but I'm ready. This scandal further solidified my intentions." He excused himself, stating he had to use the restroom, leaving her struggling to process the implications of him announcing his retirement while she was being reassigned. That would place Lynx in the position of top contender to become the next superintendent. She would be out. The board loved to promote from within, so the likelihood of them conducting a nationwide search was slim. Her stomach churned. She looked Lynx's way to see if he was celebrating.

Lynx, however, had another concern. He practically growled, "You don't have to like me, but you will respect me."

"Respect?" she snarled, glad to have an outlet for her disappointment and helpless anger. "You don't respect me, so how can you demand that in return?"

"Easy. I've never been dishonest or been a cheat. Unlike you."

Hot fury blazed, and she erupted. "For the millionth time, Lynx Harrington, I am not a cheater—but you're too much of a know-it-all to let me explain."

"I don't need an explanation for something I saw with my own two eyes."

"Whatever," she fumed. "I don't like you. And just know this—I'm a woman of my word. If you tell me to sit, I will sit. But you can't stop me from standing on the inside."

Chapter Five

Shanna knew how to make an exit—he had to give her that. She stomped out of the room after her powerful words, presumably to join his father at the press conference. In all his thirty-four years, Lynx had never met a woman who infuriated him the way Shanna Jacobs did. It had been this way for the month and a half they had dated in high school, and it was something she had mastered. Once again, she had managed to weasel her way under his skin, talking about "working under him." The woman was a major frustration, needling him with those soft inviting lips.

His revived attraction had been swift. Unexpected. Difficult to fathom. He didn't even like her most of the time.

Yet for a brief moment, Lynx wanted to taste those lips. Again. Watch the fire in her eyes burn from a different source of flame.

Lynx raked a hand through his hair. He thought of Irene Nottingham—his twenty-eight-year-old on-again, off-again girlfriend of almost two years. It had been months since they had been in the same continent.

Irene was a YouTube-channel chef and food critic. In the past year, her followers had grown, leading to more exotic opportunities. She had traveled to both Delhi and Indonesia since early April, leaving Lynx on his own. However, Lynx was not the man who would seek relief in another woman's arms, no matter how spirited or desirable she might be.

But this sudden awareness of another woman alarmed him.

Irene needed to come home.

Like, *yesterday.*

His phone chimed.

Lynx dug into his pocket to retrieve his cell phone. He had a message confirming his reservation at the Hot Springs Resort and Spa in North Carolina for Sunday night through Wednesday morning. He had organized the trip because he and Irene needed to reconnect and decide where they were going as a couple.

Now he had a second reason: Pop's watch. Lynx hadn't told anyone in his family about his quest for his grandfather's missing timepiece, but he knew his father would be overjoyed to see the heirloom returned to the family.

Irene had promised she would be back in time for his father's annual Fourth of July celebration/reunion. It was one of the few days per year all his brothers made a point to be together.

Lynx glanced at the clock. She should already be on her flight home. There were no calls or text messages.

He knew what that meant.

Since he was alone, he didn't hesitate to call. She picked up on the second ring, and he put the phone on speaker.

"I was just about to call you," she said in her sultry voice.

He greeted her before saying, "Please tell me you're driving from the airport. You promised you'd be here." Although he could tell that was not the case, judging from the loud music blasting in the background.

"Ummm, see, about that. I won't be able to make it. I have a photo shoot."

"It's been about three months," he said. "I'm beginning to think you don't want to see me." When the line remained silent, he asked, "Is that it?"

Lynx heard her yell out to someone that would be there in a minute. Then she continued. "I—I don't want what you want. I've told you that before. You want to get married and have kids. I don't see myself playing the good little wife at home or being a baby maker. I want to travel the world and that's what I'm doing."

She had said that quite a few times, yet Lynx had held on. "We can make it work. We can fix things."

"You don't get it. I know you like fixing things. I've watched you work on your watches with incredible patience, and I believe that's how you see me—a project—but there's no fixing me. I'm still the same selfish woman I was when you met me. I don't see me changing anytime soon, and honestly, I don't think you understand me enough to even care."

He sighed. There was some truth to what Irene was saying. In some ways, he did see her as a project. "What do you want me to do with your stuff?" he asked, rubbing his eyes.

"Can't you keep it for me?" she asked—a sure sign of her selfishness.

"No, I won't do that."

"Then trash it. And while you're at it, lose my number." She uttered an expletive and ended the call.

Lynx looked at his phone. *That's it, then.* He had known this was coming. He hadn't known he would feel…relieved.

Irene was right: he wasn't in love with her, but he believed she needed him. She had an unstable past, and he had been willing to offer her stability and a permanent home. However, you can't make a food critic like a dish no matter how much love and effort you put into it.

A throat cleared behind him.

"What a neat ending," Shanna jeered, coming into the room.

"Hasn't anyone ever told you it's rude to eavesdrop on a private conversation?" he fumed.

She laughed and pointed at him. "Your face is all red. I'm sorry if I've embarrassed you. I left my keys and came to get them. I only heard a woman telling you to lose her number."

"My girlfriend. Make that my *ex*-girlfriend."

Curiosity filled her eyes. "You don't seem heartbroken about it."

"We were apart more than we were together." He shrugged. "I guess we wanted different things." Lynx didn't know why he was explaining his personal life to Shanna. It's not like he was interested in her.

He scanned her from head to toe, acknowledging that she was off the scale when it came to fineness. Those curves and hips were more than a handspan. Just the way he liked it. He was always trying to get Irene to eat more than a quarter of her plate. Too bad he and Shanna didn't gel. They were like a blend of vinegar and water. Yet he asked, "What about you? Is there anyone special in your life?" His traitorous voice dropped with the question.

She raised her brows. "I don't think that's any of your business, and it's not an appropriate question to ask, considering the circumstances."

"How so?" Lynx moved closer to her, seeing a light panic in her eyes. He liked that he rattled her, enjoying their verbal sparring.

She licked her lips, curving her body into his, lighting a tiny spark within him.

"You're practically my boss. This is skirting the line of professionalism."

Her words doused the flame within him like a flyswatter on a bug. He held up his hands, moving across the room. "I apologize. It won't happen again." His tone was all business. "Would you prefer to work with one of the middle school principals instead? I can try to catch my father before he makes the announcement."

She shook her head, appearing agitated.

He had misread her body language. "I don't know what came over me just now." He had a clean record and would never usurp his authority, even though he viewed them as equals.

She placed a hand on his arm. "I'm not used to men flirting with me. I haven't dated much since college. My words were too harsh."

He searched her eyes and saw she was being earnest and relaxed…somewhat. "Thanks for explaining, but I won't *skirt the line*—to use your words—or overstep. Just because you're beautiful, it doesn't give me the right to make you feel uncomfortable. That wasn't my intention, but it won't happen again."

She lowered her eyes, her lips downturned.

Lynx dropped into one of the chairs to cover the evidence of his desire.

Patrick entered the room to put on his tie and jacket and gave them a pointed look. "The press conference is about to start. I would like you both to work on a plan of action and get it to me no later than next Tuesday."

"I'm on vacation for the next two weeks," Lynx shot back. Even though he and Irene were over, he had every intention of going to the resort. "You signed off on my request months ago."

"Not anymore," Patrick said. "I need to present a concrete plan before the board for their final approval." He rushed through the door.

"I can create a draft and email it to you, if that helps," Shanna offered, hovering by the door.

"I don't work that way," Lynx replied, trying to hide his resentment. It hadn't even been twenty-four minutes, and this woman was disrupting his life in more ways than one.

Shanna toyed with her dress. "I'm sorry. I hate being a burden. Maybe I made a mistake fighting to keep my job."

"You're not a burden," he felt compelled to say, regretting his earlier thought.

Tears welled in her eyes. "I'm the only one my mother has to support her. She gets a small disability check and an even-smaller retirement. I have to give her the best. That's what she did for me and Yanni. It's what she deserves."

His own mother had abandoned him, and if it weren't for Tanya Harrington, Lynx might have ended up a delinquent—or worse, dead—so he applauded Shanna for taking care of a mother who had been there.

A crazy idea presented itself and he was bananas enough to mention it. "How about you come with me?"

Her brows knitted. "I don't understand."

"Come with me to North Carolina. We can work through everything during the drive."

"I don't know if I'm ready for all that." Her eyes darted all over the room, refusing to meet his own. The bold woman from moments ago had disappeared and had been replaced with one who looked indecisive...and scared.

He lifted a hand like a Boy Scout. "I won't touch you. It'll be all business. I promise. You'll be safe with me. I am just ending a relationship and I have no intention of picking up where we left off years ago."

She chewed on her lower lip and tapped her feet while she considered his proposition; then she placed her hands on the table. "I'll go."

"Great. Be ready to leave Sunday morning."

"Sunday?" she squeaked.

"Yes, Sunday. We'll return on Friday. I already made reservations at Hot Springs Resort, so pack accordingly. We'll stay there for four nights, and then Thursday, we'll drive forty-five minutes to Asheville, where I'll attend a private auction, spend the night at the Omni, then return Friday." He rubbed his chin. "I'll send you the itinerary and tell you all about it on the drive. You'll enjoy yourself at my expense." Watching her face cloud over, he decided to dare her. Shanna never backed away from anything that resembled a challenge or competition. "Unless you're scared to be alone with me."

That did it.

"Never. I'll be ready." She challenged him back with a glare.

He hid his smile. "Great. That settles it. See you Sunday morning at six a.m. sharp."

Chapter Six

Shanna rushed behind the podium, trying to ignore the flashing cameras and the questions slung her way. She squinted under the bright lights. They had set up the podium in front of the building. The lawn had been mowed and the shrubs trimmed. The backdrop to her demise was picture-perfect. Even the weather was cooperating.

The crowd had grown since she had entered the district office. Vehicles of all sizes lined the parking lot, overflowing into the streets. People sat on their cars' hoods, some on the grass, but the majority stood behind the reporters.

She went to stand beside Patrick, donning her calmness like a cloak to shield herself from the prying eyes. She tented her hands behind her back and placed a small closed smile on her face to keep her bottom lip from quivering. She hoped the podium hid her shaking legs. In her peripheral vision she saw Lynx approach, and she tensed. He stood close enough for her to hear him breathing. His presence calmed and irritated her at the same time.

Patrick cleared his throat, and the crowd grew silent. The sun had eased a bit, but it was still very hot. Patrick reached into his jacket for a handkerchief and mopped his brow. He tapped the microphone and introduced himself, Shanna and Lynx before reading the statement.

"Thank you for coming out today, although I wish it under more auspicious circumstances. I will make a brief statement before allowing a few questions." He paused and looked at the crowd. The reporters nodded their agreement.

Shanna observed how Patrick commanded respect. Even now, she was learning from him.

"The school board for the Love Creek school district has been given the task of investigating an SAT scandal. The five students have been interviewed by our human resources department and our school board attorney. Their SAT scores have been invalidated, which the board feels is a more than adequate sanction. With the support of their families, the students will take the ACT exam because they still need a chance to prepare for their future careers."

Shanna seethed. The students were guilty, yet because their parents were affluent, their lawyers had made sure to protect their futures. While she was being punished despite her innocence. The injustice was glaring.

"As a result of our findings so far, assistant principals Todd Smith and Michael Houghton and three educators have been relieved from their posts. Shanna Jacobs, the principal of River's Edge High, has not been found culpable in any way related to this scandal—"

A commotion from the crowd interrupted his speech. Shanna cocked her head to see parents from her town, holding up signs demanding her resignation. She placed a hand to her mouth.

"She needs to go!"

"Fire her!"

Each time Patrick attempted to speak, they yelled. The superintendent became stern. "Enough! The board and district accept your need to express yourself, but you need to quit with your antics. Most of you have known Shanna Jacobs all your lives. Now, if you quiet down, I can continue with my statement."

Shanna stared straight ahead, refusing to appear defeated. Lynx straightened, moving close to his father, a silent show of protection, solidarity and… leadership.

Chastised, a few lowered their heads, but others hoisted their signs higher. On the inside, Shanna's heart squeezed at her townspeople's betrayal. Strangers, she could understand, but her own… That cut her to the core. Their hostility added to the tension in the air. They would never accept her as superintendent. The knowledge made part of her resolve weaken.

"Superintendent, they are allowed to express

themselves," a reporter interjected. "Has the school board allowed parents to voice their concerns?"

Patrick gripped the podium and simply stared. After a few seconds, he continued in a calm tone. "Shanna Jacobs, the principal of River's Edge High, has not been found culpable, but we will conduct a thorough investigation. During this time, Lynx Harrington will assume leadership of both River's Edge and Love Creek High. Shanna has graciously agreed to assist him in his duties which we feel is in the best interests of the staff and students."

A cheer rose from the rear. Shanna's heart was pierced by their delight over her demotion.

Patrick signaled for them to still. Once they complied, he said, "We anticipate that once Shanna has been vindicated, she will be back to her duties as principal in the fall."

At those words, the crowd chanted, "Let her go… Let her go…"

Reporters jumped in with more questions, but Shanna tuned them out. All she could hear were the voices demanding her termination. All she could see were angry brows, bunched fists and lips curled with contempt. At her.

And she had done nothing wrong.

Hurt and rage battled within her, and she bit her inner cheek to keep from bellowing her innocence to the crowd.

Patrick shifted his stance and reminded the throng that Shanna was one of their own before changing topics. "I would like to take this opportunity to announce my retirement this fall." This time the crowd moaned—a stark contrast to how they had reacted to her demotion. "The board will begin their search for my replacement, and they do hope to promote from within." That was his subtle endorsement of his son. Smart move.

But a detriment to her.

A little before the conference ended, Shanna rushed to her vehicle to avoid the mob. She was so glad she had parked a few feet away from the podium. Part of her knew she couldn't look at Lynx—her new boss—in the face. She couldn't pretend to be happy, smile through it all, while her world crumbled. She gripped the steering wheel, unsure of where to go. Her sister wasn't home, but she didn't want to have Yanni come home and see her in such a low state. Shanna pulled out of the lot and braked at the stop sign. She looked to the left and right and debated. She needed a moment of peace.

Of security.

Then an image of the perfect place flashed through her mind. She knew exactly where she would go.

Chapter Seven

This had been their hangout spot after school.

His and Shanna's when they had dated for a hot minute in high school. That's how Lynx knew where to find her.

Lynx parked his car near the town's convention center, right next to Shanna's SUV. The center was the hub where most of the major events in the town occurred. Everything from Disney dances to weddings to the mayor's funeral had taken place inside. He stuffed his hands in his pockets and walked behind the convention center. There was a trail that overlooked the water. The path led to the edge of the beach. Though there were signs posted, people swam and fished there anyway, but most chose to sit on one of the benches placed along the mile path, content to listen to the lapping of the waves against the rocks and sand.

He trekked the tree-lined path and sniffed, smelling a mixture of the sea air and funnel cakes. From where he stood, he could hear the strains of an acoustic guitar from one of the three restaurants on the beach. It was close to dusk—orange and blue hues blended together and created a beautiful snapshot of the approaching sunset. There were seagulls squawking as their wings tapped the waves, and he could make out the fins of a couple of dolphins.

Looking out for the tips of the yachts and avoiding the duck poop, Lynx passed the gazebo and paused.

There it was.

Their bench. Under the crooked streetlamp.

Shanna and Lynx had spent hours on that bench, watching the yachts go by, wishing they were in them. When they weren't boat-watching, they'd studied—and argued. They had each enjoyed trying to do better than the other. After their breakup, Lynx had stayed away because the memories had been too powerful, and he knew Shanna frequently visited the pier.

He stopped a couple feet away and eyed the lone figure sitting on the bench under the streetlamp with her arms wrapped around herself. Tiny moths and gnats flittered under the glow of the lamp. She sat still, staring into the distance at the water that looked almost black under the night. A jogger sped past her line of vision and waved, but she didn't seem to notice. Lynx raked a hand through his hair, debating whether or not he should leave her alone. But he couldn't. Especially not after that press conference. Lynx wasn't sure how Shanna had maintained her composure under the heat of the town's censure. He needed to know if she was okay.

When Shanna turned her head his way and pinned his gaze with hers, he knew she needed him, even if she couldn't admit it to herself. Lynx ambled over and sat next to her. They sat for a few minutes in silence before she spoke.

"All those years when we used to come here and share our dreams for the future—not once did I see this happening. I thought all I had to do was get a better future. I stayed in school, said no to drugs, avoided alcohol, and yet here I am. An outcast. A pariah. I did everything right, worked longer hours, and I am about to end up with nothing."

"I wouldn't go that far," Lynx said, hating the dejection in her voice. "This scandal doesn't erase all your accomplishments. You were a mentor to many young girls. Most of them are in college because of you."

"None of that matters. In this day and time, you're only as good as your last social media post. That's what I'm discovering. No one cares about the hard work I have put into the school. No one cares that ninety percent of our student population got into college because of honest hard work." She massaged her eyebrows. "I'm reduced to the five students— less than one percent—who cheated. I'm affiliated with two assistant principals who decided to pressure teachers to turn their backs and let them cheat." Shanna flailed her hands. "That's what people will remember and focus on. When they see me, they think that this little black girl was too ambitious and that if this were a man—a white man—that wouldn't have happened."

Lynx drew in a sharp breath. "I don't think race or gender has anything to do with this. This is about the scandal." Even as he uttered the words, he realized the fallacy. Too much history in the country dictated otherwise. Innocent lives were snuffed out on a daily basis. Still, Lynx hoped this town was different.

She scoffed. "Feed yourself that lie and you'll end up with indigestion. The school board is made up of three old men and two young women. All white. There isn't one person of color. If this had happened at Love Creek, I guarantee you wouldn't have been demoted and placed under my supervision."

Her bitter sentiment held a brick of truth that settled into his stomach. He shifted. "My father is black. He's the superintendent."

"Correction—your *adopted* father is black. Patrick Harrington worked his butt off without a speck of dust on his career path. He didn't give the board a reason to deny him. That's why he got elected. You are very much white and subject to the same privilege that continually eludes those of us of a darker hue."

All he could do was nod. She was right about his privilege. It was the reason why he hadn't considered how race or gender would be an underlying factor in the scandal. "I'm sorry, Shanna. I do think all this will be behind you by the fall, though." He sounded optimistic…and hollow. Lynx wasn't sure of the appropriate words to show his support, but she would have it nonetheless.

"If this were just about the scandal, it would be so much easier to handle. But all across social media, I see the comments of those who felt I should never have been given this position in the first place. Never mind that I legit earned it. They relish hiding behind the false safety of Twitter and Facebook to give me a modern-day lashing for not knowing my place. The whip has been replaced with a keyboard, but the effects are the same, if not worse. I don't know if I can bounce back from these wounds."

Lynx shook his head. "If anyone can, it's you. You're a fighter, an overcomer. It's one of your most infuriating and admirable traits." He ached to draw her into his arms, but Shanna would see that as patronizing.

"My people have continued to thrive despite enslavement, so I know I can beat this. But this isn't just about me. I have a mother and a younger sister, whom I fear will face the same censure I'm facing. This isn't fair to them. Do you get that?"

"I don't think that will happen," he said. At least, he hoped it didn't.

"Now you're being naive," she said. "When I saw the crowd outside the district office, I thought the town was coming out to support me. I thought it would be the town of Love Creek, fighting with me, rooting for me, against the nation. But they cheered—" Her voice broke. "Begging for my termination."

"People are fickle. You know that. The same people who cheer will be the same ones rejoicing when your name is cleared." He looked out at the waters. Two seagulls appeared to be gunning for the same spot, the same fish. There was a small struggle until one flew off victorious. The other went back to hunting. If only humans took this approach, life would be much simpler.

She cocked her head. "Look at you. You sound like my champion more than my competition." Her gaze narrowed. "Why are you here? Shouldn't you be off somewhere toasting your next promotion? You're practically a shoo-in for superintendent now."

He wanted the superintendent position. He wouldn't savor a win handed to him by default. "I would have preferred a bloody, glorious battle over this."

"Me too. Because if it weren't for all this hogwash, I would have gotten that position."

"Hmm. Not sure about that." He gave her a playful shove.

She lifted her chin. "I'm positive," she said, her eyes flashing.

That was the Shanna he knew and respected. He pumped his fists. "There goes that spirit. Keep it. Let that fire propel you, because this scandal will not be your legacy. We will fight it. Then you can apply in another town for superintendent."

"We?" She raised a brow, a small smile on her lips.

"Yes. *We.* Let's fix this, and then we can go back to being rivals once this is all behind us."

She gave a small chuckle and stood. "That sounds like a plan. Beating you fair and square is something I can look forward to. I'd better get home, as we have an early day tomorrow."

"Do me a favor—get some rest and stay off social media."

After making sure that Shanna got into her vehicle, Lynx drove home, deep in thought. When he had first dated Shanna back in high school, he had been a young, carefree teenager. He hadn't considered any of the repercussions of dating outside his race. If she hadn't cheated on that chemistry exam, who knew where they would be now. Because in all his years of dating, he had yet to meet someone who fired him up like she did. For him, he loved Shanna being his equal. She had challenged him and driven him to succeed. He thought they had made a great team. Plus, arguing with her was fun.

But this cheating scandal was opening up a harsh reality he hadn't considered. There were others who despised Shanna's authority for no other reason than her race or gender.

Later that night, in bed, her question about whether or not Lynx would have received the same consequence ate at him. He couldn't say for sure what the board would have done. That knowledge made his spirit ache. He folded his arms behind his head. Lynx had never wondered about what his parents might have faced because they had chosen to adopt a white son. They had loved him, and because of that, he proudly bore the Harrington name.

If they faced censure because of it, neither Patrick nor Tanya had let on or treated him or Hawk any differently. No one had ever said anything derogatory to either him or his brother...although that could have been because of the size of their fists. When it came to defending their family back in the day, their fists didn't discriminate.

He rubbed his eyes, knowing sleep would be far to come. Turning on the television, Lynx could only hope that Shanna had taken his advice and that she was now sound asleep.

Chapter Eight

Shanna had lied.

She was scared.

Beyond scared.

It was a little after ten Saturday morning, and Shanna lay in her queen-size bed, looking up at the ceiling, willing herself to get started on her day. She had gotten up earlier that morning, just before dawn, and had pruned the plants, hoping that would relax her. But all she had to show for her efforts were chipped nails and dry, ashy hands.

The thought of being alone on a trip with Lynx made her tingle with fear, anticipation or a combination of both. Her insides quivered. She would be spending hours on the road with him. Shanna doubted they could make the journey to North Carolina without butting heads, even though Lynx was determined they could be allies against the scandal. There wasn't much they agreed on for long.

Plus, she had spent the last couple of hours scrolling through social media, though Lynx had warned her not to. But she couldn't resist.

The overhead fan spun, and she had closed the door to keep the air from the AC unit circulating in her room. The temperamental central-air system pushed cool air through certain ducts in her modest two-bedroom, two-bathroom home. The entire duct system needed to be replaced, right along with the rusty twenty-year-old boiler.

Hearing a rap on her door, she called out to Yanni to enter, pushing thoughts of Lynx and the scandal aside.

Her twenty-three-year-old sister flounced into the room, wearing a robe, smelling like grapefruit. Her wet tendrils created a ring around her T-shirt, but Yanni didn't seem to mind. She had inherited their mother's olive skin tone, amber eyes and shorter stature, standing at five foot four. Like Bernice, her sister was a fireball of energy. She rarely sat still and had probably been up at five to complete her daily 3K run.

"You're finally awake," she said, plopping on the edge of Shanna's bed. Splashes of water from her hair hit Shanna's cheek. "I waited up for you until about ten or so, but I must have fallen asleep."

Wiping her face, Shanna said, "I went to the pier over by the convention center. I needed to sit by the water to think And then I drove around for a bit before stopping at the book store." She wouldn't mention seeing Lynx. Her sister would read more into that situation. Yanni knew of their feud and had suggested that their real issue was bridled passion or something like that. Her sister read too many romances.

"Yeah, this whole SAT thing is all everybody's talking about. People have been coming out of the woodwork to hit me up and ask about you."

Shanna's heart raced. She pulled herself up into a sitting position. "What were they saying?"

Her sister shrugged. "Some of them were coming for you. When I defended you, they turned on me. I was going toe to toe with some of them for most of the night. People can be real judgmental and harsh. I had to block a few so-called friends."

"I'm sorry, Yanni. This is my greatest fear being realized. I didn't want any of this to touch you."

"It's all good. I can handle it. Sometimes stuff like this makes you see what people are really made of. Who they are. Some undercover racists were exposed. Some jealous crabs in a basket were revealed. I had no problem unfriending them, because they weren't my real friends in the first place."

Her sister was quite spunky and strong. Shanna admired and appreciated her defense. "Still. I'm sorry. I'm supposed to be protecting you, not the other way around."

"I don't need protection. Besides, I'm not about to let those small-minded people ruin my good time."

Shanna then informed Yanni she would be out of town. Yanni pressed for details.

"It's a work retreat," Shanna said before divulging she was traveling with Lynx.

Yanni waggled her eyebrows and rubbed her hands. "Wait a minute. Maybe something good will come out of all this mess. He'll be the hero that saves you from the haters and trolls." Her voice sounded dreamy. "You know he's got the body and looks to play Superman."

"Listen, I don't need rescuing," Shanna said, rolling her eyes. "I've been taking care of myself for years." Although Lynx did have the signature dark hair and blue eyes…

"Still, you have needs. You know what I'm saying?" Her sister stuck her tongue out and undulated her hips.

Shanna was not about to discuss details of her intimate—or rather, lack of intimate—life with her baby sister. That wasn't happening. So she gave Yanni a pointed look and declared, "The only thing that will be happening is that I will have figured out a way of dealing with this scandal so I can get back to my normal life. I hope you'll be okay here on your own."

Giving a dismissive wave, Yanni said, "Go on and try to have a good time now that I know you'll be in good hands. Pun intended. I'll be fine. Besides, I'm planning to go to Siesta Keys with the girls." She glanced at her phone and looked at the time. "I'll be leaving within the hour."

Shanna frowned. "I thought you were coming with me to the nursing home." She slid her feet off the bed. "They're having a special Fourth of July celebration, and I offered to help out with the grilling and serving."

"Naw. I'm good." Her sister didn't meet her eyes.

Shanna took Yanni's hand in hers. "Yanni, look at me. I know what this is about. This is about Mom screaming when you went to hug her the last time we were there."

Her light brown eyes darkened. "She wouldn't calm down, no matter how hard we tried." Yanni shrugged. "It doesn't make a difference if I'm there or not. She won't remember. I can't talk to her about my life, and you can't share this whole dilemma you're going through."

Seeing the sadness mixed with worry on Yanni's face made Shanna's heart twist. Their mother's condition had worsened significantly faster than they'd expected. Bernice hadn't been lucid in weeks. She had forgotten how to feed herself and how to do simple things like tie her shoes.

"Go out with your friends." She patted Yanni's hand. "And as for my situation, everything will work out. You'll see."

"Tell her I love her," her sister said in a small voice before wiping away a tear.

"I will. Make sure you carry your sunscreen."

"I'll be fine, *Mom*."

Shanna chuckled. She supposed she did sound like Bernice, when their mother had been herself.

Shanna had had to step into those shoes when Bernice's mind began to fail. In the early stages of her illness, her mother had asked Shanna to look out for Yanni. She had, but Bernice had already laid a great foundation.

"Don't touch the platter of cookies on the counter," Shanna called out. "They're for the cookout."

"All right, Mom."

Her smile faltered, and she touched her stomach. She used to dream of feeling a child growing inside her. Her current love situation—or rather, *lack* of a love situation—dictated that wasn't going to happen anytime soon.

She hurried into the shower, groaning when the water came out lukewarm. She had to pump extra hard to get out the last of the Dove GoFresh Pomegranate & Lemon Verbena body wash. Once she was finished at the cookout, she would stop at Walmart. Shanna had been so consumed with the fallout from the scandal that she had neglected to go shopping.

She lathered herself, imagining for a moment Lynx's hand touching her in the most intimate of places. She reared back, bumping her head against the low showerhead. Where had that come from?

Shanna couldn't recall the last time she had been intimate. That could be why Lynx had flashed into her mind. Or maybe it was because her sister had compared him to Superman. For real, though, when was the last time she'd shared a shower with a man? She put on her face wash, striving to recall. It had to have been at least five years ago, and that relationship had withered after four months. Shanna was not the kind of person who would swipe right or left on dating apps. Eighteen months ago, she had enrolled in an online doctoral program. She had been focused on her courses, spending her free time writing papers, and had no time to go out to meet anyone.

All her lonely nights would have been worth it if she could have achieved her ultimate goal: becoming superintendent.

Shanna was a semester away from completing her doctoral degree. That would have given her the extra edge. But she wouldn't even be considered now. Shanna had no idea what to do with herself.

Maybe she should apply in another county, like Lynx had suggested. Her heart protested. Love Creek was home. It's where she wanted to be.

Maybe she would take off the fall semester.

Have fun.

Then get back to it.

Her breath caught. She had never been the person who deviated from a goal once she got started, and she had no idea what it felt like to not finish something. Shanna was already rebuking that frivolous thought.

But it had taken root.

And was growing at rapid speed.

Rinsing off, she grabbed an oversize luxe towel and dried off before applying a generous amount of sunscreen.

She donned a pair of white shorts and a red-and-blue shirt. Shanna grabbed the cookies, put on her sunglasses and donned a pair of denim wedges. She placed lip gloss on her lips and tucked her hair into a bun. Satisfied, she reached for her Vera Bradley sling backpack. Yanni had already left. She sent her sister a text.

Let me know when you get there.

Ok.

Slipping her phone into the small compartment of her bag, Shanna ambled out the door, avoiding the cement fountain. Its bright blue paint had long faded, and its cracks and crumbles made the former showpiece an eyesore. Standing water had made it a great nesting place for tiny grass frogs to reproduce and for mosquitoes to breed. No matter how many times she scooped out the water, the heavy Florida rains would fill it, bringing new inhabitants. It was a vicious cycle. If it weren't one of her mother's favorite pieces, Shanna would have had it removed. A secret part of her hoped her mother would get well and return home, and Shanna needed it to be there.

Once she arrived at the nursing home, she walked around the building to the back where the cookout would be held. A vibrant mix of flowers created a wonderful fragrance. The staff at the facility kept their hedges trimmed and applied a fresh coat of paint every summer. She yearned to take off her wedges so she could feel the lush grass under her feet. But of course, she didn't do that—ant piles under the grass were a strong possibility.

Making her way across the lawn, Shanna headed for the covered pavilion with enough seating for up to thirty people. Music from the '70s blasted through the double speakers on opposite sides of the space. A couple of the residents were dancing, which translated to a well-timed yet off-beat dip and sway. Their wide smiles and laughter lightened Shanna's heart.

To the far right, near the trees, one of the volunteers had already fired up the grill. She placed the cookies next to the plates and cups on a table with a checkered tablecloth. Her mother wasn't among the handful of residents out, so she knew Bernice hadn't had a good morning.

There were at least a dozen uneaten hamburgers and hot dogs. Shanna made a plate with two hamburgers, one with pickles and ketchup for her mom and another with ketchup and mayo for herself. She took two bottles of water and went to seek out her mother.

She darted through the paneled doors, welcoming the feel of the AC. The way she was sweating, she would need another shower. She stepped into the lounge area, loving how the floor shined. The microfiber couches and armchair had been artfully arranged to give it a nice, cozy feel. Soothing elevator-style music was playing, and potted ferns had been placed in strategic places.

She headed to the staircase and took two at a time. Once upstairs, she entered the hallway and went down to the last room on the right. She waved at most of the staff she knew, glad when they waved back. No one brought up the scandal, for which she was relieved.

"Bernice had quite a morning," one staff member said. "She didn't touch her breakfast, and we made her favorite. Cinnamon French toast."

She steeled herself and tapped on the door before pushing it open. The room was painted a mauve color and had two twin beds on opposite sides of the room. Shanna and Yanni had decorated Bernice's side with teddy bears, their pictures and butterflies. On the chest of drawers, Shanna had placed an artificial ribbon plant. Her mother's bedspread was also mauve, with blue and white bedding and accent pillows. Over Bernice's bed hung an oversize photo of Bernice, Shanna and Yanni.

Her mother sat in a yellow sofa chair in the center of the room with a doll hanging off her lap. Shanna had read that the doll could be therapeutic. On a good day, Bernice would dress and feed her baby. Today, the doll was naked.

Bernice was dressed in a pair of jeans and a pink shirt, though her feet were bare. At fifty-six, her mother still looked youthful, though her luxurious locks were unkempt. Shanna could see they hadn't been brushed, maybe for days. To look at her, you would never know Bernice was a victim of such a crippling illness—that is, until she spoke. Each week, Shanna could see the regression.

"Hi, Mom," Shanna said, drawing closer to place

the food on her tray. She broke off a piece of the hamburger and said, "Open your mouth."

Bernice tilted her head and scrunched her nose. "I'm not hungry."

"Mom, I heard you didn't eat breakfast. You've got to eat." Shanna's stomach grumbled.

"Why are you calling me 'Mom'?" Bernice asked, her amber eyes confused. "My daughter is six years old."

This meant she didn't recall Yanni. Shanna was glad her sister wasn't there to hear this.

"I'm Shanna," she said, tapping Bernice on the chin. "Eat a piece of this burger."

"I don't want any," Bernice yelled. "Why did you come here? Did you come into my room last night? Who are you?" With each question, her voice raised.

"Calm down, Mom. It's me."

Bernice stood, holding the doll by one of its feet. "I'm going to need you to leave."

"Okay. I won't make you eat. Just sit." Shanna took a bite of her own burger and went to the chest to get a comb and brush. Bernice eyed her with suspicion before sitting. Shanna released the breath she had been holding. Her mother appeared to be de-escalating.

She sectioned her mother's hair in two, giving it a good brush to detangle the curls before starting on the braids. It was remarkable that Bernice didn't have one strand of gray hair. While she braided, Shanna began to talk about plants. Bernice added to the conversation. Thank goodness—her mother was coming back to her.

Shanna rested a hand on her mother's shoulder. Her heart warmed, and her eyes welled. "I love you, Mom."

Bernice lifted a hand and patted Shanna's hand. "I love you, too, Shanna. Thank you for taking care of me. You're a wonderful daughter, and I'm so proud of you. Give your sister a hug for me." Then she gathered her doll and retreated into herself.

Shanna held in her disappointment. Tomorrow could be a better day. She decided to return to the cookout and help with the food.

She went over to the gentleman who was turning the hot dogs and hamburgers on the charcoal grill. The smoke from the coals filled the air. Shanna knew her hair would hold the smell and she would have to wash it later.

After greeting him, she asked, "Do you need me to help with anything? Take over the grill?"

"Naw, miss. I've got this. You'll swelter under this heat," he said. "You can help serve later. If you don't mind, I need more barbecue sauce from inside and a water bottle."

Giving him a thumbs-up, Shanna entered the building, once again appreciating the cool AC. She made her way to the lunch area and asked for the condiments. She would get the water from the cooler under the pavilion on her way back.

When she saw Lynx enter the area, her mouth dropped. He wore a pair of blue cargo shorts, a white T-shirt and sandals. A young man stood with him, whom he spoke to for a few seconds before patting him on the back. After spotting her, he sauntered over to where she stood. As he neared, she saw the T-shirt had Harrington Family emblazoned on the front in bold red letters.

"What are you doing here?" she asked. Of all the nursing homes, he had to show up here.

"I could ask the same of you," he said.

"My mother lives here, and I volunteered to help with their Fourth of July barbecue."

He raised a brow.

"Early-onset dementia," she explained, hoping Lynx wouldn't ask too many questions.

"I'm sorry to hear that," he said. "One of the young men I mentor asked me for a ride here to visit with his grandfather, who's a retired veteran."

"I didn't know you mentored." Learning that about him added to his appeal. That, and the way his muscles bulged under that shirt. She was having a hard time keeping her eyes off his lips. She needed to remember this man was her rival. He might have some redeemable qualities, but he wouldn't hesitate to best her if he could.

"I've been doing it for a few years." He ran a hand through his hair, combing it away from his face, and then smiled. "I'm all about being charitable. Some of these young men have no one to encourage them. I remember those days."

Maybe that's why he was helping her.

She was a charity case.

"I've got to deliver this," she said, holding up

the large barbecue sauce bottle. With a quick wave, Shanna took off.

"See you Sunday," he said.

She felt his eyes on her and resisted the urge to look back. After getting the water out of a large cooler and handing everything to the man at the grill, Shanna busied herself by fixing plates and serving the residents. An hour later, the music died down and the staff began bringing residents inside. That's when Shanna departed. She had enjoyed the time with the residents and was grateful for a reprieve from the scandal.

But it was short-lived.

The previous day's mail was resting on the counter in the kitchen, and among them was her sister's tuition bill. As she wrote out the check, Shanna wondered how long she would be able to provide for Yanni's education. She didn't trust the school board to honor their word. Though the board would still offer the same compensation, they could cave to the demands of the public and rescind their offer. Then she could lose her house. Her sister would have to take out student loans, but worse—her mother would be forced to leave the nursing facility.

She drummed her fingers on the countertop. Or... she could work with Lynx and outshine their expectations. The uncertainty gnawed at her, but that was her only recourse. And it was the one she could live with no matter the outcome. Shanna had proved herself once. She would do it again.

She didn't have a choice.

Chapter Nine

Lynx turned into the long driveway a little after two o'clock, admiring his parents' freshly cut manicured lawn. Their two-story home was located on the beach and boasted ten bedrooms to accommodate their seven sons. His parents had taken down the huge palm trees, choosing to keep the landscaping clean with smaller dogwood and cypress trees. They had recently painted the exterior of the house a sand color with white trim, which made his childhood home bright and cheery.

Parking in one of the spots in the circular driveway, Lynx put on his shades and reached for the three bags of ice he had promised to bring.

He walked through the front door, past the formal dining and living rooms, through the kitchen and into the oversize family room. The walls were painted a shade of yellow called Firefly and trimmed with green. Caleb and Brigg were stretched across the gray couch while Ethan lay across the checked area rug. He was surprised to see Ethan around. His brother, a former Olympian and now swim coach at the middle school, was always at the pool. All three men had their eyes pinned on the baseball game on the eighty-inch television screen. It didn't matter the sport—if a game was on, the Harrington men watched.

They jumped up when he entered, giving hugs and dap.

"Who's winning?" Lynx asked.

"The Pirates are holding it down so far," Brigg said with a yawn. He was still dressed in the dark blue uniform bearing the Love Creek Police Department logo, though his shirt was undone. Most of his days were spent at Love Creek High but he did pull night shift on occasion.

"That's what's up," Ethan chimed in.

Caleb was on his cell phone. Most likely reading a law journal.

Lynx addressed him. "Ease up today, bro."

"I will," Caleb said. "Just looking at something real quick."

The other brothers laughed, knowing *real quick* translated to hours.

"Hawk here yet?" Lynx asked.

"No. You know your brother—he's going to be the last to arrive," Brigg said.

Leaving them to the game, Lynx went through the French doors leading to the deck, which had been a gift from him and his brothers. They had also each chipped in a few grand to create a partially covered outdoor oasis. It featured wood panels, all-weather patio furniture, a dining area, barbecue area, solar panels, a hot tub that could accommodate up to fifteen people and a large rectangular pool.

He called out to his father, who was firing up the grill, and his mother, who sat on a lounge chair.

"Hey, Mom. Where do I put the ice?" he asked, holding up the bags.

Tanya jumped to her feet, then cupped his cheeks and smiled. She had on the family shirt with a pair of capris. She wore her hair short like Jada Pinkett Smith's mom and had dyed it different shades of brown and blond. Lynx thought she looked twenty years younger than a woman in her sixties.

"Put it in the cooler. I'll get it from the garage," she said.

Lynx gave her a light nudge with his elbow. "I've got it, Mom. Relax."

If he knew his mother, she had been up since daybreak, preparing macaroni salad, mac and cheese, salad and corn; and seasoning the fish and other meats. His father would grill the quartered legs and steak, more than enough for them to take home for lunch and dinner the next day. Axel and Drake would take over the grilling, though.

Lynx retraced his steps to the kitchen and walked through the door to the garage. He found the cooler in the far corner and proceeded to rinse it inside and out; then he poured the ice inside. When he reentered the kitchen, Axel and Drake were there.

Axel had on his signature shades.

"It's just us here, bro," Lynx teased. "You can take those off."

"Whatever, bro," Axel said. "You don't know what it's like." Slipping his glasses on his tee, Axel came over to give him a hug.

As Hollywood's current "it" man, Axel was in high demand. He had the height and looks that had made him *People* magazine's Sexiest Man Alive the prior year. Lynx and his brothers had ribbed on him for that cover for months.

"Where's that cute assistant of yours?" Lynx asked, referring to Madison Henry, the niece of his favorite high school teacher. He never went anywhere without her. Maddie kept Axel organized. His brother was a talented actor but would forget to brush his teeth if he didn't have Maddie by his side.

"Maddie's out there with Mom," Axel said.

"I hope you're not overworking her," Drake, ever the middle school counselor, said.

"She's fine. I pay her well."

Lynx shook his head. Axel believed money could solve anything in his life. However, even with more than enough, Axel wasn't satisfied.

Ethan walked in. "So are the rumors true?" he asked Axel.

Axel shifted. "What rumors?"

Axel's face was on all the trash mags. According

to them, he'd been to Mars, shot, hospitalized and reported dead twice.

"Are you and Natasha LaRue engaged?"

"I'm not allowed to say." Which could mean yes.

"Don't tell me she's pressuring you to commit," Lynx teased.

"Unless… you actually got bitten by the love bug?" Drake goaded.

"Who's bitten by the love bug?" Hawk boomed, coming into the kitchen. He held a large bouquet of lilies, which he placed on the kitchen island.

As the eldest Harrington, Hawk commanded all their respect, and he had earned it. He was the biggest and thickest of them all, and though he had the brains, he preferred to use his brawn in the NFL. He was known as the Beast due to the scar on his face, which they were never allowed to talk about.

"Axel. He's in love," Brigg followed behind, taunting him.

Lynx met Hawk's eyes. The brothers shared a smile. Lots of pushing, shoving and good-natured ribbing followed.

"How's it going?" Lynx asked under his breath.

"I'm almost at that point," Hawk said.

"You're really going to retire?"

"Might be time to try something new." Hawk gave him a knowing stare. "How's Irene? Still trying to fix her?"

Lynx clamped his jaw. He hated being known in the family as Mr. Fix-It. Yes, he liked fixing things, which was why he had purchased a fixer-upper as his home, but he didn't try to fix people. At least, *he* didn't think so.

"We're over," he said. "Her choice."

Hawk's eyes held respect. "Good choice. That was probably the most unselfish thing she has done since being with you. It's like I said, bro, you can't help someone who doesn't want help. She's a wild card, and she's going to play until she's all played out."

"I don't believe in giving up on people that easily."

"Like our bio mom did to us?"

"It's preferable to being jaded and bitter."

Hawk dated a stream of women, never allowing them to get too close. The only woman who had a solid place in his heart was Tanya Harrington.

"To each his own, little bro."

He cocked his head. "Don't you get tired of the game, the chase? No pun intended," he said, referring to Hawk's being in the NFL.

"What's going on with you?" Hawk asked, folding his arms.

"I just think I'm ready for something more... concrete. I want to share my life with someone and have a family."

Hawk chuckled. "No wonder Irene ran off." He must have seen Lynx's face because he grew serious. "If that's what you want, bro, I'll support you one hundred percent. I wouldn't touch marriage even if it came with the Heisman Trophy, but I wish that for you."

Tanya came inside, ending their private talk. "Y'all need to go get your father off that grill."

*Yes, ma'am*s followed by a rapid departure left Lynx alone with his mom. He dawdled on purpose, needing to speak to her.

"You all right, son?" she asked, coming to hug him close.

"Irene ended things yesterday."

"Ah, I see." Tanya led him to the kitchen table. "How does that make you feel?"

"I'm fine," Lynx said. "I wasn't in love, but I just hoped that what we had would've developed into something—more."

Tanya shook her head. "I knew from the first time I saw you with her she wasn't the one. You need the sparks, son. The first time I saw your father, I felt a sizzle—an electricity that has never diminished in all these years but has only intensified. Yes, you need friendship and trust, but Patrick does something to me that I can't put into words. That's what you want. Don't settle for less than that."

A picture of Shanna flashed before him. There was no denying the magnetism between them. But they weren't friends. They weren't even amicable. And, though he was determined to help her, deep down he didn't trust her.

However, thoughts of Shanna brought another topic into his mind. He tilted his head. "Mom, did you face a hard time raising me and Hawk?"

She narrowed her eyes. "What do you mean?"

"It couldn't have been easy adopting two white sons," he gently prodded.

Her eyes showed her understanding. She patted

his arm. "We did get haters from both sides—black and white. Our black friends felt we should have helped other black children. Our white friends felt we had no right to call you our sons." Tanya patted her already-perfect hair. "When we took you to the park or went to a restaurant, Patrick and I could feel the looks—and some did more than look. They would dip their mouth in our business." Her expression grew fierce. "But we didn't care. Sometimes we would respond, but most of the time, we just went on our way." His mother went to get a glass of water before taking a sip. "From the moment we saw you and your brother, we loved you. It might sound trite or like a big cliché, but love is love. And it does conquer all. Yes, we had some hard times, but it never outweighed or overshadowed our love. It never made us doubt our decision to bring you into our family— it strengthened it. In my heart, you and Hawk are mine. Nothing society says or feels will change that."

"You're such a strong woman," Lynx said, getting up to kiss her on the cheek.

"It's not me. It's love. You'll see and know it one day, son," she said, smiling. "And when it comes, get ready and don't ever let it go."

"I'm sorry for what you faced, but I'm happy you took us in."

She chuckled. "You're acting like we had a choice. My heart wouldn't have had it any other way."

Chapter Ten

The round Roxy Rainbow luggage Shanna had purchased online from Pottery Barn, after seeing some of her students with the piece, was splayed open on her queen-size bed. The sun had already risen at five thirty that Sunday morning, and Shanna had already showered and dressed in a tank and shorts. The only thing left to do was pack.

She emptied the laundry basket and sniffed, enjoying the smell of the lavender, vanilla and cedar from the Bounce Sweet Dreams dryer sheets. Shorts, jeans, tanks and swimsuits littered the top of her gray-and-burgundy comforter.

Yanni had called the night before to say she would be spending the night up in the Keys. Shanna couldn't blame her sister for wanting to enjoy her final week before returning to campus. Shanna folded the clothes and placed a few of them in the suitcase, along with underwear and toiletries, before putting the rest away. She dumped a one-piece swimsuit and a tankini in the case; then she went into her closet to get a couple of sundresses and matching sandals. The only thing left to decide was if she needed to slip in a few pieces of lingerie.

Purchasing lingerie was her secret guilty pleasure. About 90 percent of them still bore tags, but that didn't stop her from buying. In fact, it was time she wore them. For her. She traded out her sensible underwear for some of these pieces.

At exactly 6:00 a.m., she walked outside her door with her suitcase, some snacks and her laptop. Lynx was already parked outside. He got out of his car, and they exchanged pleasantries. She appreciated how he held open the passenger door for her and proceeded to place her stuff on the back seat.

"Have you eaten?" he asked, getting back into the vehicle.

"Not yet," she said, her heart thumping in her chest. Momentary panic seized her. She gripped the door handle, fighting the urge to run back into the house.

"Are you opposed to stopping at Dunkin' Donuts?"

"That's fine." She choked the words out, trying to overcome her nervousness.

She felt a hand on her arm. "Shanna, you'll be okay with me. I promise. My mother raised me right."

She turned to look into his blue eyes and released

a pent-up breath. "I don't know why I'm stressing about this road trip. For all intents and purposes, this is a work trip."

He gripped the wheel. "If you're not comfortable, I can call the resort and cancel. We can work on the plans, and I'll go straight to the auction."

She could tell from his tone Lynx didn't want to, so she appreciated his willingness to make the sacrifice on her behalf. Shanna shook her head. "No. You're the one going out of your way to help me. I need to relax." She eased into the seat. "Let's go."

"Are you sure?" he asked.

"Yes. Let's get on the road."

They stopped for food, each paying for their own meal at her insistence.

Once Lynx tapped off his tank, they began their trek.

She yawned and closed her eyes, feeling the effects of yet another sleepless night. Though some women would have been occupied with thoughts of the fine man beside her and what might happen on their excursion to North Carolina, she had been contemplating how to fix this crazy situation in which she had become embroiled. The board's handling of the scandal was to succumb to the public's demands at her expense.

Shanna must have drifted off to sleep because when she opened her eyes, the digital clock read after eleven o'clock. They were already in Gainesville.

Lynx looked her way. "It's about time you're up. You were knocked out."

"I didn't realize I was out this long."

"I'll be stopping in a few minutes to gas up. We'll be in Georgia soon, so we can stop for lunch if you're ready."

"Are you hungry?" she asked, reaching into the back to grab her snack bag. She took out two plums and handed one to him. "I also have grapes, cherries and almonds."

Thanking her, Lynx took the fruit and bit into it. Some of the juice ran down his chin. A foolish temptation to use her tongue to lick it off his face played in her mind, but she shunned the notion. Shanna dug into her bag for a napkin and handed it to him so he could wipe his face.

Lynx's face reddened, but he took another bite. "This is good. Much better than the gum and mints I've had."

She laughed at the wad of wrappers in the cup holder. "I'll throw them out when we stop for gas." She bit into her plum, amazed at how well they were getting along. Well, she had been asleep for almost five hours. That could be why. Nevertheless, her body relaxed at the ease between them.

He pointed at a sign. "The exit is about three miles away. I'll stop then."

Great. Shanna could use a bathroom break. She needed to wash her face. She was sure she had been drooling in her sleep. Checking her face in the visor, she wiped the sides of her mouth with the back of her hand.

They passed a field of flowers. "What's your favorite flower?" Lynx asked.

"I don't know," she said. "I'm more into plants."

She gasped at the sight of her hair. Her frizzy hair was no match for the humidity.

"Goodness. I look crazy," she said. "Why didn't you tell me?"

"You look fine. I like the sleep-tossed-hair look."

Since she wasn't sure if he meant that or was just being nice, Shanna rolled her eyes but didn't respond. She took another napkin to store both the pits of their plums. "How much further do we have to go?"

He tapped his cell phone, which was in a holder. "According to Google Maps, we have about nine hours left on our trip. If I don't stop now, there won't be another rest area for thirty miles."

She wiggled in her seat. "I'm glad we're stopping. I need to stretch."

She saw Lynx's eyes dart to her legs before he looked ahead at the road. Shanna pretended not to notice, though her stomach constricted. He was checking her out. Glancing at him from under her lashes, she caught him staring at her again.

Lynx pulled up to an empty pump at a sorry-looking gas station, Roberto's. One of the letters was missing from the name, and another letter hung like a hangnail so the sign actually read *Robet's*. The pumps could use a fresh coat of paint and the ground, cementing. But this was the only place for miles, so she wouldn't complain.

Shanna exited, stretched and dumped the trash;

then she grabbed her backpack and headed to the bathroom to freshen up. Once she had used the restroom and washed her hands, Shanna washed her face, redid her hair and applied lip gloss, careful not to make too much contact with the bathroom sink. The toilet water ran, the trashcan overflowed and the floor needed a good mopping.

She hurried outside, using a paper towel to touch the door handle. She met up with Lynx, who must have also used the restroom since his hair appeared slicked back with water.

"I'll make sure to stop at a better rest stop next time," he muttered.

"I agree," she said.

They shared a smile.

"I see you handled the bedhead situation and got rid of your drool," he joked.

"Yes, uh, I always have scrunchies in my bag for times like this," she breathed out. Her heart was racing like a young girl's on prom night. Shanna remembered that she needed breath mints. She excused herself and rushed back into the store to buy a pack.

On her way out the store, a *USA TODAY* magazine cover caught her eye. She frowned and bent over before covering her mouth. She was on the cover. Shanna looked around the store, wishing she had worn a cap and sunglasses. The last thing she wanted to do was be recognized. The *best* thing for her to do was to get out of the store.

Returning the magazine face-down on the stand,

Shanna tucked her chin to her chest and moved toward the door, but then she bumped into someone.

"Excuse me," she said.

"No problem," the Caucasian woman said, holding the door open.

Shanna raised her head to reach for the door when the woman gasped. Her eyes went wide, and her mouth hung open. "It's you," she breathed out, opening and closing her mouth like a puffer fish and blocking Shanna's path. The woman scrunched her face and pointed at Shanna, eyes filled with venom. "You should be ashamed of yourself. You need to be fired."

"Ma'am, I don't want any trouble. Please move out of my way," Shanna said in a low, calm tone. She could feel the eyes of the other patrons in the store. A couple of people hovered close behind her.

"You're nothing but a cheat, and you're not fit to be around children," the woman fired off, getting into Shanna's space. Spittle hit her face, and Shanna reminded herself that she was an educator and couldn't afford to end up in jail or on social media.

"Move. Now," she commanded in a more forceful tone—one reserved for tardy teenagers lurking in the hallways of the high school.

The woman's eyes shifted, fearful, but she didn't budge. She appeared indecisive until someone from the crowd egged her on. *Count to ten,* Shanna told herself while engaging this Petty Patty in a staredown.

"Ma'am, please vacate the store," the cashier called out.

Shanna's brows raised when she realized he was addressing her instead of the actual troublemaker. "I'm trying. Why don't you tell her to leave?" she shot back, insulted that the assumption was that *she* was the one causing trouble.

She exhaled. "This person has refused to get out of my way, and I am doing my best not to put my hands on her. She's the one who is in the wrong. Not me."

From where she stood, Shanna could see Lynx drive away from the pump. He pulled into a spot by the entrance of the store and came inside, his brows knitted. "What's going on?" he asked. Before she could answer, the other woman spoke up.

"Do it," Petty Patty jeered, with a hand on her hip, calling Shanna outside her name. Her bravado had returned with Lynx's presence. "Put your hands on me and I'll call the cops. I got all these witnesses to protect me."

"I don't want any trouble in here," the cashier yelled, his eyes trained on Shanna.

Lynx placed a hand on the woman's arm and asked her to step aside. She flipped her hair, all smiles and flirty, before moving so Shanna could pass. While he addressed the woman in a low voice, Shanna stomped over to the car, furious and mortified all at once.

After a minute of two, Lynx entered the vehicle.

"What was that about?" he asked, holding the

steering wheel. "She made it sound like you were in her face. All because she recognized you as the principal in the scandal."

"Of course she did. It was about me being a black woman in America," Shanna snarled through gritted teeth. "She called me a nasty name and practically spat in my face. Yet I'm the one the cashier tells to get out the store." Her chest heaved. She wanted to scream or throw something, but all she could do was grip the edge of the seat.

"I handled it," Lynx said, starting the car and letting it idle.

"How? By appealing to her sense of reason?" she scoffed and shook her head. "What you should have done was reach out to me. Talk to me. Not doing that cements the stereotype that I'm an angry black woman who is incapable of being rational."

His shoulders slumped. "I thought I was defusing a volatile situation, but I got it all wrong. I'm—"

"Stop. Please, don't say it," she muttered, cutting him off. "I don't need an apology. I just need you to accept what I'm going through and understand why this is more than the SAT scandal. I'm not playing the race card. Because my life is not a game. The consequences I'm facing are very real." She blinked, refusing to cry out of frustration, hating that she had to explain her pain. "I know you grew up with a black father, but I can guarantee that you didn't see the looks and comments Patrick received. The assumptions he had to overcome because he dared to love and care for someone outside of his race."

"For what it's worth, I only meant to help, not harm," he said after several tense seconds. "If you need to talk, I'm here."

"I don't want to talk." Shanna released a shaky breath and willed herself to calm down. She didn't doubt Lynx's intentions or his willingness to listen. Just like she didn't doubt the intentions of *others* of his race. They intended to use this scandal to strip her of her worth, her self-dignity and her integrity. The woman who had harassed her came out of the store and walked past their car. When she saw Lynx with Shanna, she flipped him off.

"Did you see that?" he said.

"Yes, and you didn't even do anything. Welcome to my world." She leaned back on the headrest, feeling weary. "I just need to know you're not all talk and you're really in my corner," she said.

"I'm trying to be."

"What does that mean?" she said, wrinkling her nose.

Lynx met her gaze. "Can I ask you something?" His intense stare made her break contact, feeling a shyness coming over her.

"Sure, just as long as it has nothing to do with race. Because I want to put that whole ordeal behind me. I don't want to dwell on the actions of ignorant people."

"It's not about that... Something has been bothering me for years," he said, rubbing his chin. Shanna narrowed her eyes and gestured for him to get to the point. "You're smart. You're brilliant. Why did you feel the need to cheat on that chemistry exam back when we were in high school? Were you that afraid of losing to me?"

Her head snapped up. She placed a hand on her chest as the old fury surfaced. "I can't believe you. Really? It's been fifteen years. Can't you let that go?"

Lynx's eyes widened. "You asked me if I'm in your corner. I have to address that so I can honestly answer your question."

She cut her eyes. "Just drive." If she could return home, she would, but she was in the middle of a redneck town. Gainesville was known for racially motivated hate crimes. Shanna was mad, not stupid.

She would remain in this car, but she didn't have to like it.

Chapter Eleven

Lynx drove with the caution of a man who knew if he made one wrong move, he would get cussed out. In his opinion, Shanna's reaction to his question had been like using a fire hose to put out a candle.

He couldn't be in her corner knowing he didn't trust her 100 percent. That wasn't the man he had been taught to be. Since it had been years ago, it shouldn't be a big deal for her to explain. That's how he saw it. But he couldn't drive nine hours with this thick tension in the car.

Lynx cleared his throat. "I apologize for upsetting you yet again, but how am I supposed to trust you when your integrity is questionable?"

She tapped her foot against the passenger door.

Her tapping made her shorts hike up higher on her leg. "Do you think I care what you think of me?"

"If you don't care, then why are you furious?"

"Because," her voice boomed. He heard her take short breaths before she gritted out, "I don't like being judged for something that happened when I was a kid. I can't keep reliving that with you when I have this scandal to deal with."

He jutted his chin. "A leopard doesn't change its spots."

"Good thing I'm no leopard." Her foot tapping increased. "Can we drop this?"

Clamping his jaw, Lynx accelerated. "Fine. We'll have it your way." He turned the radio on to slow jams. Taking her with him had been a colossal mistake. Maybe he should make a U-turn and get her home.

But the thought of holding his grandfather's watch kept him heading north. The very moment he changed lanes, the sky darkened and thunder cracked. Within seconds, they found themselves in the middle of a torrential downpour. This was a usual occurrence for Florida, so Lynx was experienced in driving under these conditions.

He slowed, turned on the defrost and put the wipers on at the highest speed. Most drivers had put on their hazard lights, and some had pulled over on the side of the highway. He spotted a couple of motorcyclists sheltering under an overpass.

"Maybe you should pull over," Shanna suggested in a cautious tone.

He noted her wide eyes and sought to reassure her. "We should be able to ride this out. I bet in another mile or so, we'll be back in the sunshine. Trust me."

"The way you trust me?" Shanna whispered; her animosity evident. Mindful of the traffic ahead, he kept his eyes peeled on the car in front of him, putting on his hazard lights. For several seconds, the only sound was that of the windshield wipers.

Then Shanna spoke. "I was Mr. Bloomfield's assistant," she said, referring to their old high school chemistry teacher. "The night before the test, I went home on a high because you and I had gotten into a fight about something—"

"It was a history debate that I believe I won," Lynx supplied. He remembered how frustrated he had been when she refused to declare him the winner. "You were the judge, and you voted in favor of Carolyn just to get back at me."

"She won fair and square," Shanna said.

Lynx disagreed, but he would let it go.

She continued her recount. "The best thing about that day was when you grabbed me and kissed me right in front of my locker."

He kept his eyes on the road and said, "If I recall, you initiated the kiss."

"I did not," she exclaimed in outrage. "I was a good girl. I wouldn't have done something like that."

"I know. I was just yanking your chain."

Shanna laughed. A full, throaty laugh.

He smiled at the sound. It had a sensuality to it

that led to him imagining the sounds she would make while making love.

"That was my first kiss. I ran home intending to call my best friend, Laurie, and tell her all about it. But when I got home, I found my mother distraught in a way I had never seen before. Her face was blotchy and swollen from crying, and she paced through the house, talking aloud, wondering how she was going to pay the mortgage." She narrowed her eyes. "My sister sat on the floor in the family room in tears. That night was the second-worst night of my life—my mother's diagnosis overshadowed that. The same day we kissed was the very same day my father deserted us." Shanna inhaled in a deep breath. "Needless to say, I didn't do any studying that day. In fact, I stayed up all night, holding my sister, rocking her in my arms as she cried for our daddy."

Her words drew a clear image in his mind of her distress. Lynx's heart ached for the seventeen-year-old girl who had to console both her mother and sister. It didn't sound like anyone had been there to comfort her.

"I'm sorry you went through that," Lynx said, taking his eyes off the road for a second to look her way. He noticed the tears welling in her eyes, but he had to concentrate on the road ahead. The traffic had slowed to about fifteen miles per hour.

"The next morning, I dragged myself into Mr. Bloomfield's class. I remember I avoided looking at you because I didn't want you to see my puffy eyes. I placed my books on the table, and the answer sheet fell out."

Yes. That was the moment.

He tensed, waiting for her admission while wondering how he would feel once he heard the words from her lips.

"It was the answer sheet to the other class's exam. It wasn't our exam answers. Mr. Bloomfield made about three versions of his tests, saying he was paranoid about cheating. Remember, one of my jobs as his assistant was that I helped him with grading for his other classes."

His mouth opened. "Why didn't you tell me? Why did you make me think you had cheated?"

"I didn't make you think anything. You assumed. I didn't see the need to correct you since you had already tried and condemned me. Plus, I thought you were a sore loser who couldn't accept that you had been defeated at something or that I had scored better than you on that test." Her voice held an edge. "I became valedictorian because I earned it and not because I passed that exam. I pushed all my pain aside and pressed through, and I deserved that ninety-eight in the class."

"I can't believe…" He trailed off, calling himself every kind of fool. Lynx straightened. "I'm sorry I misjudged you—doubted your character."

"You screamed some vicious words at me, made me feel like dirt and then you dumped me," she said, pounding away at his guilt. It was like she was releasing all her pent-up anger—on him. He was man enough to take it, to bear the responsibility of his part in her pain.

"My father made me question my worth, leaving us like that. Then the boy I thought I was in love with all through high school and was finally dating spurned me like I was vermin. My final days at Love Creek High were torture because somehow word got around school that I was a cheater. I heard the boos when I got up to give my valedictorian address. But I made it. I survived, and I came out on top."

If he could melt through the floor of the car and flatten himself on the pavement below, he would. "You did come out on top. Despite your father—and me," he acknowledged with much shame. "I was a boy and very competitive, but I should have known you weren't a cheater. I told my best friend, and I think he was the one who blabbed, but I did nothing to defuse the rumors." He looked her way. "Back then, I was only about winning. I had no idea what you were going through. I'm so sorry. This whole SAT scandal must feel like history repeating itself, but this time, I'm with you. For real."

"Apology accepted, and thank you." She sniffed. "I never spoke about it because to talk about it, I knew I would have to relive the agony of my father's desertion. I didn't know I had the strength to do that. But today, I know I had it within me all the time." Her voice held wonderment, and Lynx was glad there had been something positive from digging up this proverbial bone.

"You are a phenomenal woman," he said with a

great amount of awe. At that moment, the traffic began to pick up, and he increased his speed. He could see some rays beyond the clouds.

"We made it through the storm, and now the sun looms," Shanna said, referring to the past and present.

"One is left to wonder what lies ahead." He reached over to touch her hand. His heart lightened when she didn't pull away.

They crossed the Georgia line.

"So…you thought you were in love with me in high school?" Lynx asked.

"Yes. It didn't last, though," she said.

"I missed out, then," he admitted. "But my desire to win superseded everything else, and I did regret breaking up with you. I just didn't have the guts to admit it."

She nodded. "It's all water under the bridge now, so to speak. Believe me. I missed out on some relationships because I was driven. I wanted to become the best to make my father sorry for leaving. I spent less time dating and more time studying."

"Was it worth it?"

She didn't answer right away. That surprised him.

"I regret not taking the time to relax on occasion— smell the flowers. I was thinking of making some changes, having some fun. I don't know if I have the guts to follow through to put thought into action."

"You have to make time to decompress. That's why I set this trip to the resort. I'm almost where I want to be, and I'm ready to shift my priorities."

"What kind of priorities?"

He wasn't sure if he should share, unsure if she would scoff at him. But she had opened up to him. It needed to work both ways. "I still want to become superintendent, but I also want to settle down, start a family."

She leaned into the passenger door. Lynx felt the loss. He questioned why women pulled away when he opened up about the future.

It stung.

"You'd make a great father," she said, her back against the door so she could face him.

"You think so?" he asked, straightening.

"I know so. You're going to make some woman rejoice for the rest of her life."

"Thanks for the ego boost." He cocked his head her way. "What about you? What are the changes you need to make?"

She held up her fingers to list off her items. "Besides the obvious of proving my innocence with this cheating scandal, I need to get the boiler changed. I also need a new AC unit. I think I want to paint my house exterior gray with white trim, clear out a lot of the dead trees and get some landscaping done. But the most important thing of all I need to do is repair my mother's fountain. Return it to its former glory."

Lynx replayed her items in his head. "Whew. That's a lot of tasks. And a lot of money you'd have to put out."

"I'd like to restore my mother's house," she said. "Yanni thinks I'm holding on to the past and should sell, but it's part of Mom's legacy. I don't think she would want me to do that."

He was already thinking of how he could help. "I bought a fixer-upper, so I got to know a lot of people—handymen, electricians, plumbers, you name it. I can get you hooked up. I became good at negotiating."

"Thank you. I might take you up on that."

"Offer's open." He changed lanes and pointed at a sign. "Are you in the mood for Popeye's?"

"I'm hungry. I'll eat anything."

"I'll take you somewhere better once we're in North Carolina."

She gave his hand a squeeze. "I'm glad I'm here with you."

"I'm glad too," he said. "I know we've had a few bumps already, but you're great company."

"Words you think you'd never say," she said with a chuckle.

But words he knew he meant.

Very much.

Chapter Twelve

Shanna and Lynx walked into the Hampton Suite at the Hot Springs Resort and Spa close to ten o'clock. The space was decorated in shades of burgundy and gray, and she liked the homey feel. Lynx sauntered into the room with the king-size four-poster bed. Shanna placed her luggage in the other bedroom, which boasted a full-size bed. The suite had a full kitchen and one and a half baths along with a heart-shaped tub. When they'd checked in, the concierge had been quick to point out the tub could fit two people.

Both had given awkward smiles, and for Shanna, it became real that they were on a vacation together.

They had already stopped for dinner in the town of Hot Springs, so the only thing left to do was shower, then slip under the covers.

Yet she was reluctant for the day to end—or rather, her time with Lynx.

Reminding herself that Lynx was her competitor and not her friend, Shanna grabbed her cell phone and texted Yanni to let her know she had arrived. Yanni sent a thumbs-up and told her not to worry about their mother. She would check on Bernice.

Gathering her skimpy sleepwear and toiletry bag, Shanna sauntered into the full bathroom and closed the door behind her. She turned on the shower and adjusted the temperature before undressing. She unzipped her toiletry bag and took out her body wash and shampoo; then she dipped a toe under the water to test the heat level. Finding it satisfactory, she placed her full body under the spray.

The entire time she showered, all Shanna could think about was how Lynx was in the next room. Ten minutes later, she traipsed into her room with a large towel wrapped around her, drying her hair with another.

Moments later, she heard the bathroom door close, followed by the sounds of the shower. Visions of Lynx naked and wet teased her mind. Her body was in heat just from her imagination.

There was no way she would make it through the next few days without combusting. She sank onto the bed and began to lotion her body, curious what it would feel like if it were his hands instead. She put on deodorant and donned her sleepwear. The smooth satin against her skin heightened the sensations coursing through her.

The door to the bathroom opened.

Shanna froze. She craned her neck, listening for his footsteps.

She didn't know what she would do if Lynx knocked at her door. She didn't know what she would do if he didn't. This was why she avoided the dating scene. It was nerve-wracking, uncertain. It transformed the most successful women into babbling, frightened schoolgirls, waiting for the guy to make his move.

But she wasn't frightened.

Or a schoolgirl.

She was a grown woman who knew with 90 percent certainty what she desired. She wasn't the woman who backed away from a challenge—or anyone, in this case. Life was about taking risks. Putting yourself out there.

Taking a leap of faith.

Yet the 10 percent of doubt that lingered couldn't be ignored. She didn't lack confidence, but she lacked expertise. Her one sexual partner had been her first and she his, and she couldn't be sure if his praise had been due to the thrill of finally having sex or because of her efforts.

There was only one way to find out.

She spritzed herself with some of the Warm & Cozy shimmer mist from Victoria's Secret; then she finger-combed her curls with curl pudding to keep her hair from frizzing.

After washing her hands and drying them, Shanna opened the door and gasped.

Lynx was leaning against the doorjamb to his bedroom. He wore plaid pajamas low on his hips.

"What are you doing out here?"

"Waiting for you," he said, holding out a hand.

Wait a minute. His confidence jarred her a bit. "You just knew I would come?"

He shook his head. "I hoped."

His humble response made her smile. She placed her hand in his. "How long would you have stood there?"

"Maybe five minutes."

"Would you have knocked on my door?"

"No. The choice had to be yours. I knew if you wanted to be with me, you would come."

Her heart did a little backflip at his words. He understood her. Knew how she operated. That was a bigger aphrodisiac than his ripped muscles and the dark hair peeking above the line of his pants.

She beckoned him close, her heart pounding in her chest. She paused before admitting, "I'm sorry. I've got too much on my mind. I'm not ready." Her shoulders tensed. This man was surely going to call her a tease.

He spoke into her ear, causing her body to shiver. "That's okay. I can be a patient man when I want something. I don't mind waiting. We don't have to sleep in separate beds, though."

The invitation was like a rich dark chocolate muffin, tempting her to take a bite. She swallowed. Such a decadent treat came with repercussions. "I don't think that's a good idea," she said, her voice raspy.

He didn't argue, which she appreciated, but he pulled away to ask, "I know you're here to work, but I wanted to ask you something I should have asked you all those years ago."

She tensed. If he asked her about her supposed cheating on the chemistry test again...

"May I take you out on a date? A real one?"

Aww. That question transported her back to their few weeks of dating. They hadn't gone out on dates but had spent time at the park, walking and holding hands. She had to admit, she was tempted to accept his date request. "I didn't bring anything fancy to wear."

"We can go to a burger joint. I just want to spend time with you."

Shanna tilted her head. His persistence meant a lot, but the scandal was like a dark cloud that loomed over her head wherever she went. "I don't know if I can go in public after what happened earlier today."

He angled his chin. "You can, and you should. You're not the type of woman to burrow in the ground. I get that this country is filled with bigots, but you know me. You know I'll defend you even if you don't want me to."

She nodded. He would. That was cause for concern. Shanna didn't want to attract any attention. She wanted this whole thing to end. "How about we hold off? I'm not saying no. I'm saying give me a day or two to think about it."

He agreed. Touching her cheek, Lynx blew her a kiss and entered his room.

Shanna walked into hers, reminding herself that she had done the right thing.

Butterflies fluttered in her stomach, a sensation she had never experienced before, making its presence felt, expanding her, testing her…and she trembled. Like a train moving at full speed, she couldn't bring these feelings to a stop. And she wasn't ready to buy the ticket for the ride.

Quit being love-starved. A man flirts with you and you're acting like you don't know what to do with yourself. Unless she had unresolved feelings she hadn't acknowledged all these years—feelings of love?

A ridiculous notion.

She eyed the bed and sighed. Slipping under the covers, she could hear the sounds of frogs and crickets and knew she could have been hearing a different sound—the sound of her moans and Lynx's groans. Slapping a hand on her forehead, Shanna knew if she had been with Lynx tonight, it would have been physically satisfying. Still, she wasn't sure how she felt about someone who could carry a grudge against her for fifteen years. She had almost given him her heart, and he had trampled her budding emotions. No. The more she thought about it, the more she knew she had done the right thing. Her body was more than willing, but her mind needed time to catch up.

To process.

She curled into a ball. Admittedly, sometimes doing the right thing sucked.

Chapter Thirteen

He was used to being the object of her sneers. Being the recipient of her thousand-watt-smile made him feel tongue-tied. But that was what greeted him when he woke up the next morning and ventured out into the living room area. Shanna looked like she was happy to see him for the first time in years.

Lynx cleared his throat. "Let me get dressed so we can go out for breakfast."

"I started a skeleton of our action plan," she said, all business, patting her laptop. She was already showered and dressed in blue jeans, a red tee and a pair of sandals.

Lynx went into the bathroom to shower and then brushed his teeth. When he passed by, wrapped in a towel, Shanna made sure to keep her head in the laptop.

He put on jeans and a plaid shirt before going to stand by Shanna. Bending over so he could look her in the eyes, he posed a gentle question. "Shanna, are you nervous, being here with me?"

She bit her lower lip and shook her head. "I woke up this morning, and I wasn't sure what your mood would be like, especially since I... Since we... Oh—" she flailed her hands "—I'm not making any sense... I feel like we made some headway yesterday on building a friendship, and I don't know if I ruined that by not..." She shrugged.

He took pity on her, knowing and understanding her awkwardness. Lynx gave her a light tug, and she stood, stepping close to him. She placed a hand on his chest and looked at him with eyes filled with trust. The confidence on her face imprinted in his mind. He would keep that look on replay. His chest puffed, and his heart warmed.

"This is going to sound cheesy, but you're exceptional. Yesterday, for the first time in years, we rose above our feud, and I feel like we made a connection. I don't want to interfere with that. Would I have minded if we had taken things to the next level? No. You're a beautiful and attractive woman. A monk would have a hard time turning you down. But I agree with you. We need to work on being friends— shoot, how about being civil for more than an hour? Because if we can accomplish that, then we can work together until this investigation is over."

They stood chest to chest.

He could smell the vanilla and peppermint on her breath. She touched his face and gave him a smile that made his heart expand.

"We need to work on our plan," she whispered, looking up at him from under her thick lashes. Everything in her tone said she didn't want to.

Neither did he, but he was going to respect what he knew she needed. "Let's eat first, then check out the area. We can find a spot outside to work on it and continue when we get back." He held out a hand. "What do you say?"

"That's a great idea. Let's go," she said before switching her sandals for walking shoes. She grabbed her wallet and stuffed it into the pocket of his jeans.

During the drive into town—and even while eating—Lynx used every played-out trick invented to touch Shanna, and he didn't care. He rubbed her elbow. He touched her cheek. He stroked her face. And still it wasn't enough.

Every time he touched her, she gave a little smile with half her bottom lip between her teeth. It was sexy and endearing at the same time.

After breakfast, they dedicated an hour on the plans at the nearby creek and then went hiking, taking in the scenic mountain views. He enjoyed her little squeals of surprise at a spiderweb above her head and her pleasure at the baby birds with their mama. The best part of their walk was when she had clasped her hand in his and not let go. He hated that they had to return to the suite.

"I can't tell you the last time I've had a good time like this," he said, dropping onto the couch and closing his eyes to bask in the cool air. He and Shanna had trekked a couple of miles, and she had kept up with his faster gait. Lynx tended to walk fast, so he was glad she could match his stride.

"Me either," she said, wiping her face with the back of her hand. "I tell you one thing, though. It's nice to be back in the AC. It's hot out there, and the humidity is off the charts."

Lynx tugged off his shirt. He was drenched with sweat.

"That must be nice," Shanna said. "I wish I could whip off my shirt like that." She fanned herself with her hand.

One eye popped open. "You can," he said, waggling his brows and keeping his tone light. "Do you want to hit the shower first?"

"Thanks." He watched her traipse into her room and come back out, holding her clothes and other items.

Once she closed the door, Lynx strolled into his bedroom. He already felt her absence. He opened the laptop he had left on his bed and pulled up his email. When school was in session, his inbox received anywhere from a hundred to a hundred and fifty messages per day. Like most principals, he fielded questions from parents and teachers, handled disputes and the superintendent. There were also many subscriptions to leadership magazines and forums that flooded his messages.

Today, his Outlook account signaled fifteen new messages. One in particular captured his interest. Lynx pulled up a *Love Creek Herald* article. Shanna had made the front page. He scanned the contents before feeling his eyes go wide. There was a gorgeous picture of her posing with him and his father, followed by an editorial news article that was both suggestive and nasty. He shook his head. He didn't even remember when or why that picture had been taken. The editorial proved that salacious gossip trumped truth any day. Sales over integrity.

A surge of protectiveness rose within him.

He minimized the article, deciding to wait until after they worked on their plan before showing her. He didn't need her to be angry and distracted. Once she had exited the bathroom, he rushed in to get ready, appreciating the peach scent circulating in the room.

A couple of hours later, Lynx and Shanna sat together on the love seat in the sitting area. Sandwiches delivered through Grubhub had been eaten and the wrappers forgotten on the glass coffee table. Shanna had placed her laptop on a small tray.

Since she had already framed the outline of the plan earlier that morning, they had a good draft finished. Though they couldn't complete it without disagreement and bickering. In fact, he had been called bullheaded and a mule.

Lynx cleared his throat. "So, to summarize, you'll institute and oversee ninth-grade academies and staff at both schools. You will also incorporate a CTE pathway at River's Edge and monitor the financials. I will supervise tenth through twelfth grade and oversee all testing. Our working relationship will consist of weekly Monday-morning meetings, where we will discuss any staffing or parenting concerns. Did I miss anything?"

"No. That sounds about right." She stood and stretched. "No offense, but I hate having to answer to you."

"None taken," he said, admiring her nimble physique. "Now, I know the circumstances aren't ideal, but I'm looking forward to working with you."

She appeared to struggle, like she was thinking how to formulate her words. "I wish I was working with you by choice and not circumstance. Not that I would choose to," she said with a chuckle.

"I hear you. If it weren't for this situation, we would still be throwing daggers at each other during leadership meetings."

"Put yourself in my shoes. If you were going through this, how would you feel?" she asked, rubbing her toe into the carpet. "Honest answer."

"I'm not as brave as you are, and I have more pride than common sense."

She blushed and averted her eyes. "I would have resigned if I didn't have a mother and sister to consider. Pride is secondary to priority."

He felt ashamed and got to his feet. He went over to her. "You're right. I'm thinking like a single man. If I were married or had other responsibilities, I'd do what I'd have to and keep my job. I was hoping that Irene—" He stopped, unsure of the etiquette of bringing another woman into the conversation.

"No need to stop on my account. I know you had—*have*—a life."

Lynx wasn't about to talk about Irene, no matter how cool Shanna claimed she was with it. "I'm ready to fall in love, get married and install the white picket fence."

"How do you know you're ready?" she asked.

He rubbed his chin. "I'm at the brink of where I want to be professionally. I want someone to share my success with me."

"I get it," she said, doing that half-bite thing with her lip again.

He shifted gears, snatching her close to him, hoping she would allow the embrace. Her body melded into his like she had been waiting for him to do this all day.

"What do you want to do for dinner?" he spoke into her hair, loving the feel of the soft curls against his face.

"Anything. I'm open," she whispered, tilting her head at an angle. A silent invitation for him to kiss her.

He had to oblige. He kissed her lips before using his tongue to lick her ear and behind her earlobe, loving the moan she produced. He placed tender kisses on her neck and cheeks before capturing her mouth. She was ready to tango. It was as hot and sweet as he remembered. He could kiss her like this for hours.

Overcome, Lynx broke off from the kiss and put

a few feet between them. His chest heaved, and he drew in deep breaths. "I'm sorry. I've got to stop unless you want to take things further."

She shook her head. He could see her uncertainty and that, if pushed a little, she might cave to the intense waves of attraction between them. Then a memory hit.

He slapped his forehead. "There's an article you need to see. I got so caught up with enjoying your company, it slipped my mind," he said, his voice hoarse. "Give me a second. I've got to show it to you."

"I'm not understanding," she said hazily.

Lynx strode into his bedroom to get the laptop. She was right behind him. He maximized the page and turned it toward her.

When she read the words, her eyes went wide, and her mouth dropped.

Chapter Fourteen

Principal Jacobs's Secret Scandal Exposed

"Why are you just showing me this?" she sputtered, telling herself to count to three. *One...two...* It wasn't working.

"I needed to keep you focused on our plan and what we can control," he explained.

"Do I look helpless to you?" Shanna raged, pacing from one end of his bedroom to the next. "You should have shown it to me as soon as you saw it."

"It's filth."

"It's my reputation."

"It's garbage," he said. "A cheap sales tactic."

"Yeah. At my expense." She took the laptop from him, her desire squashed by the words on the screen, and sat on the edge of his bed. "I can't believe an editor approved this nonsense," she mumbled. "I hope my sister hasn't seen this."

"Your sister knows you better than to believe a word on that page."

She continued to read the contents, then snarled. "They're painting me like I'm hiding something or being shady. They're implying the cheating was all my idea and how it is strange I get to keep my job and how it must be because of my close association with you and your father, that the district is sweeping this under the rug." Tears brimmed in her eyes, and she sniffled to keep them from spilling over. "All because I talked about having a high percentage of seniors pass their SATs. I can't believe this."

River's Edge High had boasted that 98 percent of its students were college bound, with the SAT scores to prove it.

"That's why I don't get why your APs cheated to help boost performance records. They didn't need to."

Lynx came over to sit next to her. She rested her head on his shoulder, grateful he was there and that she wasn't alone. The sun looked like it was about to set, and if the clouds were any indication, rain loomed.

All the hours spent in after-school tutoring and working with athletes, paying teachers stipends to provide remedial lessons in math and English language arts, offering dinner so kids could stay late to study—everything she had done meant nothing right now.

She dragged her fingers through her hair. "I busted my butt to get those scores."

"And you deserved them," he said, wrapping his arms around her. She welcomed his strength and his words, spoken with such certainty.

"Are you saying that to be nice?" she asked, furrowing her brows. She couldn't be certain that Lynx hadn't brought her here to distract her, make her vulnerable, trust him and then slide into the superintendent position once she had lowered her guard.

"I spoke the truth. If you hadn't been my competition, I'd have commended you. I was impressed with all you've achieved in such a short time. I'm sure there are many people in this town who love and support you."

His eyes reflected sincerity, and Shanna shoved her suspicions aside.

"Thank you. That means a lot, coming from you." She shook her head and groaned. "I have received some encouraging emails, but they are dragging me on social media. I'm going to become a household joke or something."

"I think you should stop going on there. You're torturing yourself and worse. Someone's going to say something that's going to irk you enough to respond. Anything you say can be misconstrued and might backfire on you. I know this seems lame, what I'm about to say, but this will pass." He kissed her forehead. "Let's get out of here and get some dinner."

Thunder cracked.

"I'm not hungry," she said.

"You have to eat."

He sounded like he cared. Shanna allowed the wonder of that to fill her heart—a heart he had already begun infiltrating after just one day. Droves of emotions pushed their way inside. Drawing in a deep breath, she pushed out of his arms, needing to put space between them.

These emotions were too soon. Too fast.

"I've got to use the bathroom," she said, skittering out of the room.

Once inside, she leaned against the door and touched her chest before releasing a plume of air. She faced herself in the mirror. "You need to remain in control." She couldn't afford to read more into his concern. Promising herself to guard her heart and not get snared by his charm, she squared her shoulders, flushed the toilet and washed her hands. When she exited, Lynx was standing by the front door of the suite, his keys in his hand.

"I'm going to get us some food. Then we're going to plan our day tomorrow and have some fun."

The rain was pouring outside, and the thunder sounded like the angels were bowling in heaven. "You'll get wet."

"I'll survive," he said with the cutest smile.

Her heart tripped; she was already forgetting all her warnings. It was like all the feelings she had buried when they were teenagers had resurfaced and multiplied. Seconds later, he was through the door.

Shanna busied herself with tossing out the garbage and tidying the living area. Then she sank into the couch, eyeing the laptop and twiddling her thumbs.

Giving in to the urge, Shanna went on Twitter using Yanni's account. Her mouth dropped. She should have heeded Lynx's advice and never gone on there. River's Edge High was still trending, with thousands of tweets and nasty hashtags demanding she be fired. Goodness. This onslaught on her character would never end.

She rubbed her temples. The school board was going to demand her resignation. It was inevitable. If she couldn't work, she was going to have to find a job in another town and sell the house. Worry ate at her at the thought of having to leave her hometown and move her mother from the nursing home.

"Keep calm. Keep calm. Keep calm," she said in a shaky voice, her heart thumping loudly in her chest. She inhaled and exhaled, inhaled and exhaled to even out her breathing.

Shanna typed in *Austin Greer*, the twelfth grader whose admission had started all this mess, and scanned his page. He was enjoying his ten seconds in the limelight even though his scholarships had all been rescinded. The ignorance of the young and wealthy. He bragged about his upcoming TV appearances and called her out to say something, to prove her innocence.

She slammed her laptop closed and counted to three, then five, then ten. She wanted to scream, to yell, to put her fingers on the keyboard and lash out; but she knew the strongest response was to provide none. She didn't have to prove her innocence. Not when she wasn't guilty.

Lynx should have been back by now.

Slipping off the bed, she ambled over to the window and peered outside. Darkened clouds and flashes of lightning filled the sky. The rain hadn't eased up. Another couple sloshed through the puddles, holding hands and laughing. She watched them, envious of their ease with each other. The rain couldn't dim their sunny dispositions. The woman stood on tiptoe to kiss her beau, unconcerned that her hair was plastered to her head and her jeans would become heavy and cumbersome.

Her heart squeezed.

Lynx's words about wanting a family came back to her. She, too, wanted someone to share her life, her bed, her dreams. Her heart.

She heard the door jangle and scuttled over to the door, widening her lips into a smile.

Lynx entered with two bags. One was tied closed, and the food was packed in foam containers, which she took from him. The other had an eight-pack of water and bottles of juice. Once he had put the extra beverages in the refrigerator, they worked together to lay out the food on the table. He got the plates; she got the cutlery. He reached for the glasses, and she poured their drinks. They moved with a rhythm like they'd been doing this dance all their lives. A dance she found she would be more than happy to press Play on and repeat over and over.

That scared her but not enough to make her stop anything she did.

They sat across from each other while they ate their meal from the Spring Creek Tavern. Lynx had ordered the Cajun Philly Melt and the Kickin' Chick'N Sandwich along with two house salads. He cut both sandwiches in half and placed them on their plates.

Her mouth watered at the smell of the blackened chicken, mushrooms and onions drizzled with a homemade sauce. She picked out the onions, took a bite and closed her eyes.

"This is good." Licking her lips, she opened her eyes to see him staring at her.

"Wait until you try the melt," he said. "The meat is tender, and it has just the right amount of seasoning."

She took a bite of the Philly Melt next and had to agree. "Delicious. We have to go back there before we leave."

"I'm glad you think so, because there aren't too many food choices in the few places to eat up here."

She nodded. "I'm good. Most days, I carry the same sandwich or salad to work."

Once they had finished their food, he wiped his mouth and asked, "So what are they saying on social media?"

Her eyes went wide. "How did you...?"

"I would've done the same thing," he said.

"I can't forget how brutal they are. Vicious. Ev-

erybody wants me to pay for something I didn't do."
Then she expressed her greatest fear. "I'm worried
the school board will change their minds and I'll be
out of a job."

"They won't," he said.

"How can you be so sure?"

"My father's a man of honor. He'll look out for
you…and so will I. We're both in your corner."

Hearing him say he would look out for her put her
mind at ease somewhat. "I feel guilty being here,
having fun, with all this turmoil. Like a president
who decides to go golfing in the middle of a national
crisis. It doesn't look good."

He patted her hand. "No one knows you're here.
It'll be fine."

His quiet confidence gave her the strength to push
her problems away and take in the beauty of the resort. The next day, they went white-water rafting and
got massages. Shanna was scared of paparazzi finding their location but Lynx encouraged her to live in
the moment. The best part of their adventure, though,
was their conversations, though she was careful to
make him do the most talking, not quite trusting
him yet. Shanna discovered something new she liked
about Lynx a few times that day.

It was easy to relax and enjoy the idyllic setting, basking under Lynx's attention. He had again
asked her out on a date for later that evening. She
had agreed. When they returned to the suite, each
had returned to their individual rooms to get dressed.

Shanna donned a black sundress, pinned her hair

and applied light makeup. Her heart pounded in her chest. She was already anticipating the night before it had begun.

Chapter Fifteen

Lynx felt like he was reliving his teenage years. Nervous, sweaty hands gripped the steering wheel. He was going on a date with Shanna. It had only taken close to two decades.

She wore a little black sundress, her long legs on display. Her feet were in a pair of strappy gold sandals and crossed at the ankles. He wore a pair of gray slacks and a black polo with yellow stripes, so their outfits were coordinated.

"Where are we going?" she asked once she had found a station that played jazz, keeping the volume low enough so they could talk. Lynx hadn't taken her for the jazz type, and she confirmed she wasn't, stating however that the music made for nice background music while they drove.

"There isn't much around here, so I found something in the next town. It's about an hour away. So I hope you're not too hungry."

She patted her stomach. "I'm good. I'm looking forward to tonight. I'm so glad we finished the plan. Did you send it off yet?"

"Yes. I emailed it to my dad for his review, but I'm sure we covered everything."

She shook her head. "If someone had told me a couple weeks ago that this would be my life, I would not have believed them."

Just then, a plop of rain hit the windshield. He frowned. "Can you pull up the weather app? I didn't see anything about rain." Another hard plop hit the glass before the rain descended in a huge whoosh.

"I don't think we need a weather app," she teased, pointing out the window. "It's coming down."

"I need to know if it's raining in the other town."

She pulled up the app and began tapping on the screen. "It looks like it's going to rain most of the night until the next day."

"This weather changes so fast, I can't keep up." Lynx used both hands to guide the car around a sharp curve. He was glad there weren't any other cars on the road, because the sky had darkened considerably since they had left the resort, and there weren't a lot of streetlights.

He leaned forward and squinted. "I don't know what's up with the weather on this trip, but it is messing with my plans."

He could see lightning flashing ahead. His instincts told him to slow down. A few seconds later, one-half of a tree fell.

Shanna gasped. "Did you see that? Oh goodness. I've never seen lightning do something like that. At least, not up close. Maybe we should turn around."

"I think so too." Lynx pulled over and executed a U-turn. He took his time driving back, shoving down his disappointment at how his date was going. Thunder cracked, followed by another flash of lightning. They both heard a huge boom, and then the electricity shut off.

"What happened?" Shanna whispered.

Lynx reached for her hand and gave it a squeeze. Then he put both hands back on the steering wheel. "I think lightning might have struck an electrical plant." He turned on his high beams. "It's a good thing we didn't go too far."

"Oh no. That means we're going back into darkness," she said. "Let's stop at a drugstore or a Walmart and get candles and other supplies."

"I'm sure they have some in our room," Lynx said. The heavy rain had tapered down to a steady drizzle. "Our room has every single amenity I can think of, so I know they must be prepared for all kinds of weather situations."

Her head turned his way. "How sure?"

A few minutes later, Lynx pulled into the parking lot of a small market. The owner must have had a back-up generator because it shone like a beacon in the darkness. Maybe the resort also had one. They rushed inside, and Lynx snagged one of the small shopping carts at the front of the store. No one else was inside but the owner at the front desk, who greeted them with a wave.

Shanna went to find the restroom while Lynx searched for the candles and matches. Then inspiration struck: there was a fireplace in their suite. Maybe he could salvage their date night. He rushed down the aisles and grabbed some marshmallows, chocolate and graham crackers. He had seen bouquets of flowers near the register.

This was the sort of establishment that also sold food. Normally, Lynx avoided eating from these places because he couldn't be sure how long the food had been sitting out, but he couldn't be picky tonight. He asked the owner to bag up some hot dogs. Shanna returned, holding bags of chips in her hands. When she saw the items in his cart, her brows raised.

"Wow. What's all this?" she asked.

"It's called making lemonade out of lemons," he said. "Or in this case, s'mores out of a ruined first date."

She chuckled. "I think it's *sweet*." He laughed at her pun. Her beaming face buoyed his spirits. He loved how she was willing to roll with the unexpected and still have a sense of humor.

Once they had returned to the resort, which was without electricity, Lynx worked on kindling the fire while Shanna lit the candles. They had called the

front desk, who confirmed that there was a generator but only for the kitchen. They said that the lights
should be restored in a few hours. The temperature
had chilled some, so Lynx knew the fire would make
things cozy. Since it was summer, he would keep it
going long enough for them to make their s'mores.

"At least the rain stopped," Shanna said.

"This weather is so unpredictable," he said, shaking his head. "It was supposed to rain all night."

She scrunched her nose. "That's why they call it
a *prediction*. You know, being a weatherman is one
of the few jobs where you can be wrong all the time
and still be employed."

He cracked up. "You are so right. We went into
the wrong professions."

He placed the flowers in a vase and filled it with
water before putting it at the center of the table along
with their hot dogs. He went to the refrigerator for
juice.

"I'll get the plates," Shanna said after bringing a
few of the candles to the table. The lights from the
candles and fireplace created an intimate setting.
Once she returned with plates and cups, Lynx and
Shanna had their meal and crunched on potato chips.

Afterward, while Shanna cleared the table, Lynx
went to work on the fire, tossing a few logs into the
fireplace. Once he had a good fire going, he went to
the linen closet for a large comforter and laid it in
front of the fireplace. Then he gathered their ingredients to make s'mores. He went into the kitchen,

glad to find metal tongs because he hadn't thought about that earlier in the store.

"Let's go snuggle by the fire," Lynx said, holding out his hand.

"I'm down for snuggling." Wetting her lips, she gave a little nod, then positioned herself in the center of the blanket.

Lynx joined her. "Do you want to make s'mores?"

She shook her head before lying down. "Not right now. I'm full from our dinner." She turned on her side and stared into the fire, playing with the locks of her hair.

Lynx stretched out behind her and drew his body closed to hers. When she didn't resist, he inhaled her scent of apricots and vanilla. She molded her body against his larger frame. If this woman didn't stop wriggling against him, he was going to explode.

Shanna turned, and Lynx gave her a tentative kiss. Once their mouths made contact, they went wild. Their tongues engaged in a frenzied dance as their passion rose. She wrapped her arms around him and pressed deeper into the embrace.

Lynx ended the kiss and spooned her against him. "I can't wait to do more than hold you."

"I want that too."

He ran his hands down her body. "In time, my sweet."

"Thank you for being patient with me." She cuddled into his chest and closed her eyes. Lynx respected her enough to keep his needs at bay. He touched her cheek, admiring her beauty as she slept. Then his eyelids grew heavy.

He must have fallen asleep because when he opened his eyes, he saw that it was three o'clock. The fire had died out, and the electricity was back on.

Shanna was moaning in her sleep, which was a serious turn-on. He hoped she was dreaming of him. Lynx ran his hand down her face and arms, luxuriating in the feel of her soft skin under his palm.

His mouth watered for another taste of her deliciousness. Her scent intoxicated him, but he maintained his control. She was a woman worth waiting for. When she opened her petal, her flower would be glorious.

Lynx yawned. If someone had told him last week Shanna Jacobs would be asleep, snuggled in his arms, he would have laughed.

But this felt natural.

Right.

He couldn't say that about most of the women he had been with. In fact, he usually preferred to sleep alone even after making love. Cuddling was not a priority, thus the reason why he had rented accommodations with two rooms if Irene had come with him. However, with Shanna, he felt a sense of ease sharing his space with her. He knew though his back would protest in the morning if he didn't get into a bed. Scooping Shanna in his arms, he traipsed into his bedroom and placed her in his bed.

It was like…she belonged.

That was his last thought before he joined her and fell back asleep because the next sound he heard was his alarm going off at six a.m. He got up and found his cell phone on the kitchen counter. The birds were up and chirping. Then Lynx recalled the space next to him in bed had been empty.

He found her typing away on her laptop on the bed in her room. She was dressed in a coral tank and shorts. The color complemented her skin tone.

"I didn't hear you get up," he said. "I'm usually a light sleeper."

She gave him a forced bright smile. Her lips looked glossy and ripe, ready to be kissed. "You were snoring hard. I tried not to wake you."

She avoided his eyes.

Lynx cleared his throat. "Shanna, do you feel any remorse about any of our interactions since we've gotten here, or are you embarrassed by anything we've done?"

She shook her head. "No. I'm more than fine with what we did—and didn't do. I just wasn't sure how things were supposed to be this morning. I didn't know how to act after spending the night next to you. I didn't expect to fall asleep in your arms." Her cheeks took on a rosy hue, her shyness apparent.

Lynx took her hand in his. "If you must know, you're the only woman in our school district I've ever kissed. I make a point to date women outside of the educational field to avoid any potential conflict. I usually sleep alone. Even in a relationship, I make a point to keep separate bedrooms. But you're the exception."

"Why am I the exception?" she asked. It was like she had no idea of her desirability. Even now, he struggled with the strong urge to make physical contact.

He shrugged. A question he would mull over later. "I don't know. You just are."

Chapter Sixteen

Every fairy tale has its ending.

Shanna dreaded her return to her reality, having treasured this time away with Lynx. Today was their last day at the resort, and Lynx had convinced her to go zip-lining. The sun was out and the temperature was returning to a balmy eighty-eight degrees.

Lynx had gotten up early to go run, but Shanna decided to get some extra sleep and call her sister. She had been in contact with Yanni via text message. Shanna was already showered and dressed. Lynx had said he would return with breakfast. She opened the sliding door and stepped out onto the small balcony, enjoying the cool morning breeze. Seeing it was a couple minutes after seven, Shanna decided to see if Yanni was awake.

"You'd better have a good reason for calling me at this hour in the morning," her sister croaked out.

"Sorry to wake you. I figured you'd be up by now. I'm calling to see how things went with Mom and to make sure you watered the plants."

"Yes, I watered the plants." She could hear her sister yawning on the other end. "I did go see Mom, but they said she was having a bad morning. They couldn't get her to settle, so I left. To be honest, I got scared. I didn't want to see her like that, but when I called later in the day, they said she was doing better. She had even drunk her supplement."

Shanna's stomach tightened. Guilt for having fun while her mother suffered filled her being. "I'm sorry I left you to deal with that."

"Quit apologizing," Yanni said, sounding more awake. "She's my mother as well. You have been shouldering this for years—I can step in for a few days. Don't spend the rest of the day worrying about her. You pay good money, and she's receiving the best care this town has to offer."

Wow. Her sister's maturity surprised her and warmed her heart. "Thank you, sis."

"How's the weather been?"

"There's been a few thunderstorms but overall, it's been great to get away."

"And how are things going with Lynx?" Yanni asked.

Shanna weighed her words. "It's going well. He's not what I thought he would be…"

"Is that a good thing or a bad thing?"

"A good thing," Shanna said. "I am enjoying his company. We worked on a plan together that I think is the best solution until this scandal is resolved." There was silence on the other end. Shanna realized their call had been disconnected and her sister was calling her on FaceTime. She pressed the video button.

"I had to see your face," Yanni said, looking alert and excited. Her hair was spread out in a huge pouf. "Yep. It's just like I thought. You're glowing."

She knew her face had reddened. Touching her cheek with her free hand, Shanna said, "I'm not... glowing."

Yanni pursed her lips. "Your eyes are shining, and your voice is filled with joy. You're in a happy place, and I think Lynx has a lot to do with it. So give me all the deets."

"Sorry. Not about to do that." Yanni pouted with disappointment. Shanna blew her a kiss and changed the subject. "Guess what I'm doing today?"

"Working? Isn't this a work retreat?"

"We finished early," Shanna said. "Lynx is taking me zip-lining."

Yanni's eyes went wide. "Oh my goodness. No, you aren't. Who is this? And what have you done to my conservative sister?"

Shanna chuckled. "Pray for me."

"You'll be fine. Make sure you take pictures—no. They can record you while you're up there and send it to me. I can't believe you're being so adventurous."

"I know, right? No one is more surprised than me. Believe that."

Yanni touched her chest. "He's good for you."

Shanna smiled. Maybe he was. She just knew she loved being in his presence enough to do something crazy like allow herself to be pulled hundreds of feet into the air, suspended by just a cable.

"I'll talk to you later," Yanni said. "I have another call coming in."

"Talk soon."

Lynx returned soon after that with breakfast. Then, after gathering her courage, Shanna zip-lined across the treetops. It was such a thrill that she went higher. And higher. Even higher than Lynx.

After their adventure-filled day, Shanna told Lynx she preferred to stay in and use the hot tub to soothe her sore muscles. They ordered their dinner using Grubhub. She showered and changed into her burgundy bathing suit and slipped under the bubbles. Lynx was dressed in a pair of black trunks, giving her a full view of all he had to offer.

Her breath caught and the hairs on her flesh rose. She had no complaints.

His toned body was tanned from the sun. She scooted over, trying to appear unaffected, but she quivered with anticipation. He stepped into the hot tub, coming to sit close to her, moving with panther-like grace.

Their bodies touched.

A shock of electricity flowed between them. Shanna knew it wasn't because of the water.

Their mouths had been in motion all week.

It was time for a different kind of conversation.

The charge between them intensified. He placed a finger under her chin and turned her head to his.

"These few days with you have been among the best of my life. And the hardest. I mean that in every sense of the word," he said. "It's been a sweet torture."

She nodded and admitted, "For me too."

She saw the desire raging within him. Her mouth hungered for another taste. Lynx leaned in slowly, like he was giving her the opportunity to back away. Shanna closed the space between them.

"I'm ready," she said.

Lynx cradled her head and crushed his lips to hers. She opened her mouth, inviting his tongue. He explored the cavern before she straddled him and took control of the kiss.

His eyebrows shot up when she changed positions, but he kept up with her groove and opened his mouth. Her tongue dipped inside. He groaned before lifting her tankini top, freeing her best features.

Cupping them in his hands, he said, "Exquisite."

His face held fascination. She chuckled. "You're acting like you've never seen breasts before."

"I've never seen yours. They're beautiful," he ground out.

He began to love on her like he had no intention of ever stopping. Her nails dug into his back as she fought for control. Lynx kept it up until she pushed him away.

Shanna hopped out of the hot tub and held out a hand. "Let's take this inside the bedroom."

She walked ahead of him, but Lynx snatched her close and wrapped his arms around her.

Heedless of the puddle of water forming around them, he placed a kiss on her shoulder before trailing kisses on her neck. She tilted her head to give him better access and moaned.

Yes. It was like he was reading her mind. She closed her eyes, molding her body into his.

His hand journeyed down her flat stomach, then lower. Shanna turned and kissed him hard. Sensations rocked through her, and her body heated, screaming for release.

Their kiss intensified, and their bodies danced together.

Oh yes, she remembered this familiar tune.

Lynx swung her into his arms and placed her on the bed. "If you're not ready, stop me now," he said, chest heaving.

She turned on the lamp and watched him watching her as she shimmied out of her bottoms. In a flash, Lynx joined her. Together they rode the waves, reaching fulfillment. Ecstasy. Completion.

Then, to her surprise, he took her there again.

And again.

Chapter Seventeen

She lay on her stomach with her bare bottom perched in the air. Lynx hated to wake her, having kept her up most of the night, but they had to arrive at the auction to purchase his grandfather's watch by eleven o'clock. It was five thirty, and he had showered and dressed in a pair of slacks and a polo shirt. He had also checked his email to see that his father had approved their plan before packing his suitcase.

He bent over to kiss her. She stirred before turning over and propping up a leg. He watched her focus on him before giving him a sexy smile—the kind that made him want to toss his clothes to the floor.

And he would've if it weren't for the fact that after a decade of searching, his grandfather's watch was within his reach.

"We've got to get on the road," he said. "You can get more sleep in the car."

"All right. I'm getting up."

She yawned and stretched, and he groaned. Goodness, the woman had no idea what she was doing to him. Or perhaps she did, and she was tempting him on purpose.

"I'll go get breakfast," he said, tearing his eyes off her glorious body and heading out the door. The sun was already out and making its presence known. Today was going to be a scorcher, but thankfully, there was no rain forecasted.

A few minutes later, Lynx parked in one of three available spots and entered the diner, holding the door open for an older gentleman to go before him. There was a hodgepodge of tables and chairs and barstools that could accommodate about twenty people, max; but every one of those seats was filled, and there was a line to check out.

"I'll be right with you," a waitress hollered, giving him a toothy grin.

He waited in line, and when it was his turn, he ordered two breakfast meals consisting of waffles, scrambled eggs and turkey bacon. He had worked up an appetite loving on Shanna, and he was sure she, too, would be feeling ravenous.

He pictured her taut body and glanced at the clock, performing some calculations. Maybe if they hurried, he could get a quickie before they checked out. Just as quickly, he nixed the idea. He enjoyed building her up to a climax and he aimed for her to experience that every time.

The server returned with his order. She couldn't be more than eighteen years old and had bright yellow hair, the exact shade of McDonald's golden arches, with red streaks. When she handed him his meal, she gave him a flirty smile. He averted his eyes and gave her a generous tip before dashing out of the restaurant.

When he entered their suite, Shanna was already dressed in a white sundress with green and pink flowers. She had put up her hair in a bun, and to Lynx, she looked serene and beautiful.

"I'm all packed," she said.

After placing their food on the table, Lynx scurried over to capture her in his arms. "I've been dying to do this all morning," he said before kissing her. She smelled like vanilla and spice, and her lips tasted fruity.

When he pulled away, she placed a hand over her mouth. "Keep kissing me like that, and we'll be late for the auction."

He chuckled. "I know. I couldn't help it. You're a vision."

She blushed. "I'm still the same me you've known all your life."

"You can be with someone for years and never truly know them." He pinned her with a gaze. "Believe me when I tell you, I'm seeing you, and I'm loving everything I'm seeing."

"Quit messing with me. I can't think when you

talk like that," she said, flailing her arms like she was embarrassed at his words.

"It's you. You're my inspiration."

She laughed. "You're such a flirt."

Lynx let it go, though he spoke the truth. He didn't mention it again, but the entire time they had breakfast and engaged in small talk, he was enthralled. Caught up, so to speak.

After they finished eating, Lynx walked through the suite to make sure they hadn't left anything behind—chargers, cell phones, underwear—before they departed. There was barely any traffic on the highway. Lynx relaxed and put on cruise control.

Shanna took a Kindle out of her bag and began to read.

"What are you reading?" he asked.

"A book on leadership," she said. "That's what I do for fun," she added before returning to her book.

Enjoying the quiet in the car, he took that time to reminisce over the past few days. He liked that Shanna was as assertive in the bedroom as she was as a principal, and she wasn't hung up about her weight. If he had to guess, he would say she was a curvy size twelve or fourteen.

In fact, she loved herself. He had spotted her admiring her dress, twirling this way and that in the mirror with a smile, which was a turn-on. Her flair and confidence added to her appeal. It was quite… freeing.

Plus, her intelligence stimulated his mind to a level he didn't think possible. He found her ideas for the high school innovative and couldn't wait to work with her.

Though he was tempted to continue thinking about her, Lynx shifted his thoughts to his grandfather's watch. If everything went the way it should, he would be driving back home with that prized possession.

Shanna put her Kindle away when he stopped for gas. He was at half a tank, but this gas station advertised the lowest price since he'd begun the journey. After using the restroom, she bought water, cashews and honey-roasted peanuts for them to snack on the rest of the way. He had about twenty minutes to go.

"So tell me about this watch," Shanna said, munching on a handful of the nuts.

"It's a family heirloom," he said. "My grandfather, Pop, told me it was made in Liverpool, England, in about 1835 or so. It's eighteen-karat gold, open-faced, with an encrusted silver rose in the front. There's a special marking on the back, which reads *James Harrington II.*"

"Wow. It sounds impressive and beautiful."

Seeing her genuine interest, Lynx continued. "Depending on the wear and tear, it could be worth anywhere between ten and fifteen thousand dollars."

"Whoa, I had no idea." She took a sip of water. "How did he lose it?"

"He didn't. He had to sell it when his family fell on hard times. When he was telling me the story, I saw my grandfather cry for the first time. I promised him I would get it back for him one day." Lynx wiped his brow. "I wasn't able to do that before he died, but I have every intention of keeping my word. That watch will be back in our family for the rest of our lives."

She touched his hand. "I think that's wonderful, what you're doing."

"Pop took me under his wing and taught me everything I know about watches. I repair and sell antique watches as a hobby. I've even returned some to other families when I could."

"Do you ever keep any?" she asked.

He nodded. "I have about ten that I refuse to part with and one special watch I handcrafted for my future wife."

"In place of a ring?"

"No. In addition, It's also eighteen-karat gold, rare and encrusted with diamonds."

"You know what," she said with awe, "I like you. I think you have a good heart, and I'm praying you get your grandfather's watch today."

"I like you, too, and thank you for the good thoughts. I'm afraid to get my hopes up, but—"

"They're already up?" she finished.

He chuckled. "Yeah. My heart is beating fast, and I can hardly breathe. Have you ever wanted something so bad, you don't know how you'll react once it's in your hands?"

"Yeah," she said, lowering her head and smoothing her dress. "Except what I want isn't achievable unless God works a divine intervention."

Her tone diverted him from his grandfather's watch. "What do you want?"

"My mother back," she said with a sniffle. "I wish dementia hadn't taken the best mother in the world from me."

His heart ached for her. "I'm sorry for the pain you must feel."

"Since her diagnosis, I've seen her rapid deterioration, but I still have hope she'll come home. I think that's why I haven't fixed or repaired things in that house. Part of me is trying to leave it just the way it was when she left though Yanni nags me constantly to do the repairs."

Lynx squeezed her elbow, having to keep his eye on the road. "Does she remember the house?"

"No. She barely remembers me at times," she said with a shaky laugh. He could see her struggling to keep her emotions under control. "I'm afraid to do something to make major changes to her house. What if a miracle happens and my mom is able to come home when I've made all these changes? She might not recognize the place."

Lynx understood her struggle. He could see she was stuck in her grief.

"I didn't have a good biological mother, but I'm blessed with a good adoptive mother, as you know. If it were my mom, I know she would want me living under the best conditions. I think your sister is right, and you should make the repairs. Preserving her house is taking care of her legacy."

He watched her consider his words before she

added, "You might be right. Take the fountain in my front yard—it was Mom's favorite thing in the world, next to plants. I got my green thumb from her. But that fountain needs cementing and rebuilding. I think I'll look into getting it restored. I also need to repaint the exterior, fix the HVAC, the boiler… The list goes on…" She leaned over to kiss him on the cheek. "Thank you for listening and for your advice. My sister will be ecstatic to learn I'll be starting the repairs."

"You're welcome. But I can't take all the credit. I don't think this conversation would have gone this easy if you weren't ready."

"I guess you're right. I'm glad I had you for a sounding board, though. I've been wondering what the best thing was to do."

He felt she knew it but just had to accept it.

"Listen to your heart," he said. "That's the best advice I can give. It won't ever steer you wrong."

Chapter Eighteen

Shanna didn't know Lynx could be so sentimental. His softly spoken words resonated in her heart and mind. The past few years she had been operating off sheer panic and in survival mode. It was time for her to take control of her mother's legacy. She liked the way Lynx had phrased that.

She felt like a boulder had been hoisted off her shoulders. After their chat, she took a small notepad out of her purse and jotted down the items she would repair. She ended up with a lengthy to-do list.

She decided to tackle the interior first. The exterior could wait.

"Thanks again, Lynx," she said, putting the notepad away once he had pulled into a parking space in the auction lot. "The repairs should have been a no-brainer, but I realize I was scared to move on and make these decisions without Mom. Doing that makes it real she's not coming back. Ever."

He was a great listener, and she liked him a lot. Well, her feelings might be deeper than like, but that was all she was prepared to acknowledge.

"I think you just needed a nudge," he said. "But you're welcome."

He exited the car and came around to open her door. She grabbed her purse and placed her hand in his. A shock coursed through her entire body. She bit back a gasp. Her heart was finding its voice and was most insistent on being heard.

"Are you okay?" he asked, bending to peer at her.

"Yes," she breathed out, fanning herself. "I forgot how hot it is out here after being in that cool car."

He narrowed his eyes and studied her for a beat, but he gave a little nod and led her inside. Shanna emitted a small sigh of relief that he had accepted her excuse. Luckily, he couldn't read her heart. She needed time to process.

The auction house was a good distraction. Shanna wandered the aisles, examining all sorts of relics, ancient and modern. There were clocks of all sizes and shapes, furniture, wall art, sconces, toys and dresses. Her eyes didn't know where to focus, there was so much to see. It was a thrifty shopper's delight and had something for every price range. There were about ten other people in the store who she presumed were also there for the auction.

Lynx wandered off to look at the watches and

jewelry in the enclosed case while she went to the dress rack. Looking through the dresses, Shanna found a vintage hand-beaded wedding dress made of lace and silk. If she had to guess, she would say it was from the 1920s. Shanna dreamed of the woman who must have worn this dress and dared to picture herself wearing it. She eyed the two-hundred-dollar price tag and pursed her lips. It was well within her price range. And her size.

She placed it against her body and strutted over to the long mirror. The ivory color complemented her skin tone. She smiled at her reflection, envisioning her hair pulled up with a pearl comb and layered curls. She would have a bouquet of lilies and baby's breath.

"You're going to make some man happy in that," a woman holding a toddler on her hip said. "When's the wedding?"

Shanna froze. "I'm not… I… Sorry. Excuse me." She darted away from the woman and rushed back to the rack to return the dress, ignoring the pang she felt inside. It was foolish to purchase a dress when she didn't even have a proposal.

Or a fiancé.

Or a man.

What she had was a week-long fling. A night with Lynx did not make him a boyfriend, no matter what her heart said.

She went to Lynx's side. He was busy studying a gold watch under a microscope. "Is that it?" she asked.

"No. Pop's watch is in the back where the auction will take place. The owner said this wasn't repairable, but I bet I can fix it." He examined the timepiece with careful scrutiny.

She looked at her watch. "It's ten minutes until eleven o'clock. We probably should head back there."

A small, ruddy man approached. "What do you think?"

"I'll take it," Lynx said, pulling out his wallet and taking out his Amex card.

Shanna envied the ease with which he had made that decision. Her mind churned over the dress.

"If you can get it working, you'll probably be able to sell it for at least twenty-five dollars." The gentleman took Lynx's card and swiped it. The approval came within seconds.

Lynx nodded. He jabbed her elbow. "Did you see anything? My treat."

"No, I'm good," she said, shifting and not meeting his eyes. To accept his offer would feed her heart's fanciful wishes, and she needed to stay grounded in the real world. But she did take a business card, and when Lynx went to secure their seats, Shanna snapped a photo of the dress.

She made her way into the auction room. There were five other men and a woman present. Shanna checked out the competition. The woman looked like a hippie with her long rainbow skirt, yellow blouse and wedges. Her hair was dyed a deep burgundy, and she sported purple lips. Shanna dismissed her.

Four of the men were dressed in casual polos

and slacks, but one of them she dubbed Mr. Distinguished. He was in his fifties, with a Charlie Chaplin moustache, dressed in a brown three-piece suit and a light brown shirt and tie. His brown shoes shone without a speck of dirt present.

Lynx was seated in the front row on the left, and Mr. Distinguished was on the right. She wasn't surprised at Lynx's seat of choice. She knew from her years dealing with him that he wasn't the kind of person who would take a back seat on the roller coaster. Then again, neither would she. They both would be sitting together in the front row for a roller coaster ride.

Speaking of roller coaster rides…his lovemaking skills might be addictive. Every time he smiled at her or touched her, she remembered where his mouth and hands had been, and she wanted more.

The owner cleared his throat and began the auction. Shanna hurried to sit next to Lynx. The first watch up for sale had several bidders, and she found the process fascinating. The owner went through the specifications before showing pictures of the watch in question using a projector and a display screen. The watches were rolled out with reverence and kept in glass cases in the center of the aisle. She sat at an angle so she could study the faces of everyone in attendance.

Some held practiced indifference, and others had bright, wide eyes. Then the bidding began. Paddles lifted as the announcer rattled off the starting bid. Watches found triumphant new owners for exorbitant sums. Lynx sat relaxed and calm through it all. When his grandfather's watch came up, he leaned forward but otherwise kept a poker face.

Mr. Distinguished scooted to the edge of his seat, paddle gripped in his hand. Shanna's heart rate increased, and she gave Lynx's hand a squeeze.

The bid started at a thousand dollars. She had to clamp her mouth closed or her jaw would be on the floor. She had no idea an old watch could solicit such a steep price.

Within seconds, a war ensued. She twisted around, knowing she was wide-eyed. It seemed as if everyone in the room intended to get Lynx's watch. None of them seem fazed by the starting price. Fortunately, most dropped off at the eight-thousand-dollar mark. Soon, the numbers inched up to $15,000.

"$15,500," Lynx called out, holding up his paddle.

She wiped at the sweat on her brow and inhaled deeply to keep from hyperventilating. It was now up to him and Mr. Distinguished.

The older man slid a glance Lynx's way before growling, "Twenty thousand dollars."

Lynx's shoulders slumped.

She tapped his shoulder and prodded him to bid.

"Thirty thousand dollars," Lynx shouted. His voice boomed in the otherwise silent room.

The tension tightened, taut with friction. The announcer looked between the two men and raised a brow.

After a beat, the older gentleman stood and lifted his chin. "Fifty thousand dollars."

Shanna's audible gasp filled the now-quiet room. She reached for Lynx's hand, but he bunched his fists and shook his head, caught up in the moment. She felt the disappointment emanating off his body and pursed her lips when she felt herself tearing up.

The announcer's voice faded, and in her subconscious, she heard the older man claim Lynx's grandfather's watch. She looked up at Lynx from under her lashes. He knitted his brows, and the muscle in his jaw ticked, but he remained in control. Once the auction ended, his stern countenance made others clear a path as he moved toward the exit.

She scurried after him, struggling to keep up with his longer strides and scared to be left behind. When he got to the door, Lynx held it open for her, and she breathed a sigh of relief. At least he hadn't forgotten her. He even made sure she was safe inside the Audi before shutting the door.

Then he got in, slammed his hand on the wheel and said, "I failed."

She rushed to assure him. "You didn't fail. He outbid you."

He appeared to be fighting back tears, and she wasn't sure if he had registered her words. "All these years of searching to lose it like this. Unbelievable."

"There will be another chance," she said, touching his arm.

He flinched at her touch before saying one word: "Don't."

She removed her hand. Tears welled in her eyes,

but she blinked to keep them from overflowing. "I was only trying to help."

"*Help* me?" he scoffed, turning to face her. "Why don't you help yourself? Great advice from the woman who's stuck in a time warp and refuses to accept her mother's condition."

Shanna told herself to stay calm, even as his words pierced her heart. This was his disappointment talking. But her mouth had its own mind. "That's real childish, Lynx. You're lashing out at me all because you're a sore loser. Always have been. Well, be warned—don't take your anger out at me. I'm not a dartboard, and I'm not going to sit here and let you say whatever you feel like saying to me."

"I speak the truth," he said, jutting his jaw. She could see from the look on his face he wasn't going to back down or apologize.

"Wow." She placed a hand over her chest. "I'm sorry I ever confided in you. I thought you were a friend, but I see how very wrong I was. My mistake. It won't happen again."

"Fine." He started up the car and tore out of the parking lot, heading to the hotel.

Shanna fumed the entire way, calling herself all kinds of silly for sleeping with Lynx. Not silly enough to wish she hadn't had sex—she had needs. But silly for thinking things could be more, for imagining she might be…in love.

Because she wasn't.

Ten minutes later, Lynx pulled up to an arching driveway to the main entrance of the Omni Grove

Park Inn. She let herself out and grabbed her luggage, ignoring the lush landscaping and the quiet elegance of her surroundings. Once inside the lobby, she scurried across the marble floors and walked up to the concierge desk.

The young lady behind the counter gave her a wide smile and spoke in quiet tones. "Hello. How can I help you?"

She tossed her hair and asked, "Yes. I'd like a cab to the nearest airport."

Chapter Nineteen

Lynx pulled into his driveway early Friday afternoon, exhausted and drained. Shanna hadn't deserved his attitude. She must have felt that way, too, since she'd bounced as soon as they arrived. He had used valet parking and caught her exiting through the door before jumping in a cab. She had ignored his text messages and phone calls, and he couldn't blame her.

Instead, he had checked into the luxury suite; then he spent hours tossing and turning in the large bed before checking out at 4:00 a.m. to begin the long, lonely journey home.

He felt every single hour she wasn't by his side.

When he wasn't grieving the loss of his grandfather's watch, Shanna filled his thoughts.

Lynx sat in his car, looking at the four-bedroom house before him—a house he had gutted and rebuilt to mirror his dream. Every detail of the interior and exterior had been selected after careful thought and research. The exterior had been painted Creamy Mushroom; the trim and shutters, Red Pepper. The black mulch around the shrubs lining the circumference of his house added a stark contrast. He paid someone to keep the lawn trimmed and maintain the landscaping, and he appreciated the results.

He sauntered into the backyard, which led to a clear view of a lake filled with sea bass and, of course, alligators. The sky was a brilliant blue and the clouds a brilliant white. He never got tired of the view. This was what peace looked like. The alligators used to come onshore to cool off under the trees, until he had hired a couple of men to cut them down. The only tree left was an orange tree, laden with the ripened fruit. He had already given his parents two bags full and taken some to the office, but it was still producing. He ventured close to pick one. On the outside, the fruit was a mix of orange and brown. He knew from experience that it would be sweet. He used his thumb to poke a hole and tear off the outer skin. When he took a bite, the juice ran down the side of his face. The sweet substance made his fingers stick together, and he savored every morsel. Lynx picked a couple more and used the crook of his elbow to wipe his face.

He swatted at a mosquito before deciding to go inside. Walking past the lanai and resort-style lawn furniture, Lynx returned to the front and entered his house. He took off his shoes and ambled across the white tiles into the oversize kitchen. He had installed granite countertops, stainless steel appliances and soft-closing cabinet doors. The sun streamed through the huge bay window, providing natural lighting.

Once he had washed his hands, he retrieved his luggage, making sure to take out the watch he had purchased and place it on the kitchen counter; then he stripped out of his clothes, leaving a trail across his living area. He needed to shower.

Wearing only his underwear, he traipsed into the master suite and stopped short. His gaze moved past the deep gray walls boasting two large pieces of art in the colors of mustard yellow, white and black; then he zoned in on the woman sprawled across the tufted and upholstered California king bed.

Irene.

She had tossed his coverlet on the floor. He walked over and picked up the blanket. After placing it on the bed, he shook her awake.

"Hey. I came in a few hours ago," she said, giving him a smile. She scanned his body before she curled into a seductive pose. She pulled out her ever-present cell phone from under the pillow, pouted and took a selfie. Then she asked, "Care to join me?"

Another woman came to mind, and if she had been present and uttered those words, he wouldn't have hesitated to join her. With Irene, he felt nothing. His desire for her flatlined, and there was no reviving it.

"Care to tell me why you're here?" He strode to his chest of drawers and chose an oversize football jersey. He pulled it over his head and stuffed his arms through the sleeves, then put on a pair of jogging pants.

She sat up and swung her long legs to the side. "I got here about an hour ago and fell asleep waiting for you to return." No, she hadn't come up into his house, acting normal, as if she hadn't cussed at him and broken things off. Irene was one bold, selfish woman.

"I'm going to need you to get out of my room, get your stuff, and get out of my house."

She came up to him. He noticed her eyes looked tired and puffy, and she looked gaunt. "I need a place to stay. Just for a few days."

"Thanks for letting me know, but you can't stay here."

Her lips quivered. "I got into an argument with the director on set, and I lost the gig. My agent is saying I might lose everything. I just need to lay low for a couple of days."

"Am I not speaking English?" he fumed. "Check yourself into a hotel." He couldn't chance Shanna showing up with Irene here.

"I don't have any money," she said in a low voice, which tugged at his heart. Irene made a sizable income, but she didn't manage her funds correctly. She spent money before she got it, which always placed her at a deficit. Lynx had bailed her out many times, with her promising to repay him. She never did. Still, he couldn't see her on the street.

And she knew it.

He exhaled. "One night. In the spare room." He refused to call it her room anymore. "Better yet, I can put you up in a hotel room."

Her shoulders slumped. "So just like that, you're over me? You didn't miss me even a little?"

"I've had months of withdrawal," he said. To agree he hadn't missed her would be cruel. Shanna's legs wrapped around him had been his therapy, his haven. He had felt a completeness with her he had never experienced with Irene.

"Did you ever love me?" she asked, toying with a tendril of her hair.

"I know you're not speaking of love. What did you once say to me? *Love is like the wind. It comes and goes.*" His brows knitted. Irene wasn't herself. He wanted to ask what was going on with her but couldn't risk getting sucked into her sad song.

"I can't feel something for you that I have yet to feel for myself." She moved to sit on the edge of his bed.

Nope. This was out of character. Something was up. "What's the real reason you came back here?" he questioned.

The tears came swift, trekking down her cheeks on a well-known path. Calling himself every kind of a fool, Lynx went to sit next to her.

"I met someone," she said before patting his hand. "I'm sorry to hurt you by telling you this."

He wasn't hurting but held his tongue to keep from enlightening her. "Go on," he said gently.

"He's one of the photographers the agency hired to tour with me." She hiccupped. "It started out as a fling. It meant nothing. Just a way to pass the time."

Her careless words stunned him. He wondered how long their "relationship" had been one-sided— or if they had been in a relationship at all. She had tried to tell him she wasn't that woman. She didn't want to be a wife or a mother. He hadn't wanted to accept her truth.

Or his.

There was no electricity between them. What they had could be likened to an opened can of soda: they had lost their fizz months ago. But he had held on.

"Then I found out he was sleeping with another girl, and I didn't expect to feel…to feel heartbroken. I don't understand how he could do that to me and of all people, with her. She isn't prettier, and she's fat. I mean, really fat. What does he see in her?" She fell apart, her shoulders shaking, snot running down her face. He retrieved a box of tissues and handed it to her.

Lynx felt an odd urge to laugh—not at her but at himself. Like he was trapped in an episode of *The Twilight Zone* and didn't know it. Only Irene would come to him for comfort because of another man. Her selfishness couldn't be categorized. And she expected him to house her.

"You were so right," he said, more to himself than to her.

"What do you mean?" she asked after blowing her nose.

"You're not ready for a relationship. Even now, you speak of love, but what you're actually expressing is disbelief, anger that a man would want another woman over you. Your heart isn't damaged—your pride is."

She dabbed at her cheeks. "Of course it is. If he's going to cheat on me, at least let it be someone who is a step above me. Not a puffer fish. His choosing her over me is humiliating."

Lynx shook his head. He couldn't believe he had considered marriage with someone so shallow. He went into what used to be her room. He had chosen a shade of blue called Tahitian Sky with white trimming and had decorated the room with blue and silver accents. Her perfumes and cosmetics littered the top of her chest. Designer shoes spilled out of the closet and lined one of the walls. Her clothes had been crammed into the small space, but Lynx had been adamant against sharing his space with her.

Deep inside, he must have known this wouldn't last.

He grabbed her suitcase, placed it on the bed and began to pack her clothes. It was time for her to vacate his residence. She was like a cat; she would land on her feet.

"I thought you said I could stay here," she said, coming into the room. "Is this because I was honest with you? You shouldn't ask for the truth if you can't handle it."

This woman was clueless. Like a hangnail, it was time to cut her loose.

"No. This is because you have worn out your welcome. You need to leave." He steeled himself, prepared for her meltdown, but she surprised him.

"Fine." Irene huffed, eyes blazing, "I won't stay where I'm not wanted." She tossed her cosmetics in a tote and gathered her stuff.

A few minutes later, he zipped the case closed; then he called a taxi.

"Where am I supposed to go?" she asked, dragging her feet and luggage to the door.

"You're grown. Figure it out." His phone beeped. "The taxi is five minutes away. Don't keep him waiting."

Her temper flared. "You're going to miss me. And when you do, don't call me or expect me to come running."

"My key?" he asked, holding out his hand.

She gave him a look filled with venom before digging into her purse for the key. She threw it, hard, and it spun across the tiles, landing outside his workroom.

"You're going to feel my absence more than you realize. But after this, I won't be available."

He didn't know how he was keeping his laughter at bay. He clasped his hands behind him and shook his head at her tantrum, allowing her to have the final word.

Head held high, Irene sailed through the door, slamming it hard for dramatic effect, which was wasted on him. Her departure felt like freedom and sunshine rolled into one.

What a week this was turning out to be.

Tiredness cloaked him like a cocoon, but he was too wired to take a nap. Lynx took a much-needed shower and donned a pair of sweatpants and a T-shirt. He returned to the kitchen to get the watch he had purchased from North Carolina and then bent to pick up his spare key. He strolled down the narrow hallway to his workroom. Out of the four rooms, this space was one he had left with the wood paneling, painting the room a light brown.

At the center of the space was his gigantic work-table with his tools neatly stacked to the side.

There was also a hutch for his prized watches. He had a space for his grandfather's watch, which he hadn't been able to fill. His shoulders slumped. Turning his head toward the painting of Pop on the wall, he whispered, "I didn't get it."

His only way to handle the guilt was to distract himself with another project. Placing the watch on the worktable, he began his inspection, but Shanna crowded his mind. After a few minutes, he decided to give her a call.

When she didn't answer, he sent a text.

She didn't respond.

Lynx wouldn't let that deter him. He knew what he wanted, and he was going to put all his efforts into getting her back.

Chapter Twenty

"So let me see if I've got this right: Mr. Fine as Can Be, Lynx Harrington, rocked your world, gave you multiple orgasms and you left him because he caught an attitude over something that had nothing to do with you?" Laurie said.

Her best friend propped a long leg on the shaky patio table in Shanna's backyard and shook her head.

Shanna gave Laurie the side-eye before taking a bite out of her Jamaican beef patty. They had stopped by the local Caribbean store after Shanna had picked up Laurie from the Love Creek airport. Both had purchased two patties each and DG Kola Champagne sodas. During the forty-minute drive to her house, Shanna had told Laurie all about the past few days with Lynx.

"I'm beginning to think I should have left you stranded at the airport."

Laurie giggled. "I'm only stating it as I see it," she said, not the least bit remorseful.

"You have a warped way of seeing things. He snapped at me, and that wasn't cool."

"He suffered a huge disappointment. You could've let it slide." Her friend bit into her patty and closed her eyes. "*Mmm.* This is so good."

"It's too early in the game to let things slide. His behavior is what I see as a red flag."

Laurie grew serious. "I think you're overreacting. It's not like you're talking about a complete stranger. We've known Lynx since forever. He's a good man—a good man who made a mistake." She wagged her finger. "There's no perfect man, but there is one who is perfect for you. Don't forget that. So stop hiding in this house."

Shanna tore off a small piece of the crust and tossed it Laurie's way. "This house has been a haven to you when you had to hide out after breaking some guy's heart. Like today. You went to Turks and Caicos as an engaged woman and returned solo, without Craig in tow. I've stated my case and rested it."

"I thought Craig was the one," she said, more than a bit defensive. "And you know why I'm picky. Cooper needs a great role model to guide him."

"My godson just needs your love. Nothing more," Shanna said, sipping the Kola Champagne. Laurie had gotten pregnant with Cooper in college when she was twenty-one. Her parents had cut her off, forcing her to drop out of school. Shanna's mom had allowed Laurie to move in with them. Laurie had then worked two jobs, reenrolled in school and finished her fine arts degree in creative writing. She was now a literary agent with her own firm, working with some of the nation's top-selling authors.

"He'll be glad to know Craig and I are done when he returns. He didn't like him at all." Every summer, Cooper went to California to spend time with his father, Paul Mansfield. He was the first of her broken engagements, which he'd deserved.

"I have to agree with Coop," Shanna said.

"Let's get back to you," Laurie said. "I think you need to answer Lynx's text messages."

"Nope. I'm done." Shanna avoided Laurie's eyes and focused on the overgrown brown grass. The shrubs and trees needed trimming.

"You're forgetting I know you. You're scared."

"Puh-leeze. What do I have to be scared of?" she asked, though her heart was racing.

"You have feelings for him. You always have. That's why you're running—because they are back in full force. You're not running from him. You're trying to outrun your heart."

Shanna rolled her eyes. "How do you come up with such corny phrases?" This time, she zoned in on the weeds that looked like trees. Great pretenders. She needed to dig them up. Anything to keep her mind off the truth—which was that Laurie was right.

"It takes special talent to spin words the way I do, and I get the big bucks to prove it." Laurie reached over and wrapped her fingers around Shanna's arm. "Honey, you laugh at me for jumping into relationships, but at least I'm swimming. You won't even get into the water."

"Ummm, I think I did more than that these past few days. I did the backstroke, the breaststroke. All kinds of stroking."

The women cracked up.

"That you did," Laurie said. "But you're not the type of woman to sleep around without getting attached. He did more than get inside your kitty kat. He's in your heart. He has been since high school, and I don't think that has ever changed."

Shanna nodded. "I do feel something. Lust. Nothing more." She sprang to her feet and walked to the front of the house, stopping by the fountain.

"Why are you afraid to fall in love?" her friend asked, coming to join her. "You dream of becoming a mother—and I'm not saying you need a man in your life to do that, but you're not the kind of person who would be happy using a sperm donor. You need a connection."

"Everyone I love eventually leaves," she confessed. "My father left when I was in third grade, and he hasn't reached out to me since. And my mother is here physically, but she's gone." Shanna broke into sobs. "She's gone, and she isn't coming back."

"I'm here," Laurie said. "I've loved you since preschool, and there's no getting rid of me. You're family. Plus, you have Yanni."

Shanna nodded, wiping her face.

"You can't stop life from happening, love," Laurie said, hugging her. "But it doesn't mean you stop living. You have to take a chance, keep going—because every once in a while, life gives you a moment. A moment worth keeping. For me, that moment was when I became Cooper's mom. He gives me meaning. But to get those moments, you have to put yourself out there."

"I don't know if I can."

"Your heart knows."

"It's too soon," Shanna said, shaking her head. "How desperate would I be to fall for someone just because he gave me a good time in bed?"

"Please don't sell yourself short," Laurie pleaded. "You have more depth to you than that. And that's why I know this scandal will be resolved and you'll be reinstated to your position as the big boss on campus."

Shanna nodded. "I need this drama to end. Like, yesterday. I had to stop checking my emails at work today because people have nothing better to do than to attack me for something I didn't do. One of the parents whose child cheated on the SAT had the nerve to say that it was my fault for not managing my staff properly. She said I needed to make sure I hired honest and competent workers, because now her child's SAT scores were invalidated. Can you believe that?"

Laurie's head snapped back. "Wow. So she's blaming you for her daughter's cheating? That is bananas."

"You don't know how badly I wanted to go off on her. But I know better than to put what I was thinking in writing. So I hit the delete button."

"That is unreal. I'm so sorry this is happening to you," Laurie said with empathy.

"How am I supposed to ever lead again after this? Even if I am cleared, I feel like I'm always going to be under a microscope and my every action will be scrutinized."

"Isn't it already?" Laurie asked. "Be real. This was your daily life as a black woman in leadership, increased to the umpteenth power. I get it, too, so I know about that life. Every time I meet with a top client, I can see their mouths drop or their eyes go wide to see it's a black woman in charge. Then I see them recover, pretending as if they weren't shocked. Some have even walked away from deals, saying they will get back to me, and I know it's because they didn't feel I could do the job."

"You know and I know the truth, but it doesn't make it hurt any less. These people are attacking my character, my race, my gender. No one is thinking about the thousands of other students I helped." Shanna wrapped her arms around her friend and sighed. "I should get you home. This isn't going to be solved today. And you're probably jet-lagged."

"All right. But promise me you'll think about what I said about Lynx. He's one of the good ones."

"I will."

She drove Laurie home. It wasn't hard to keep her promise. On the way back, Shanna replayed her entire time with Lynx, admitting she missed him with a fierceness that surprised her. She missed his smile. His touch. She even missed arguing with him.

Shanna exulted in the fact that he desired her.

That he missed her, if his texts were any indication.

This thing between them was intense, electric, making her heart palpitate with excitement and… fear. To be with Lynx, to give him her heart, would give him the power to crush her once he was done with her.

No. She couldn't take a chance, even knowing she would recover. She was a strong woman, but part of her would be forever broken. She couldn't deal with that uncertainty.

Chapter Twenty-One

Battling two major disappointments over one weekend would have led another man to drink. Lynx chose another path. He pumped iron in his home gym, and he ran. He had clocked an estimated twelve miles in total over the past two days. While he ran, he did lots of thinking and reflecting on his bad behavior.

Now it was finally Monday morning, and he sat behind his desk, tapping a finger on it, waiting to see Shanna strut into his office like she owned the place. He had a hundred emails to answer, but he couldn't concentrate. He needed to see her, make things right between them. Lynx tucked his hair behind his ear and eyed the clock. She was due in at 7:00 a.m.

At exactly 6:58, Shanna flounced into his office wearing a pumpkin-colored jumpsuit and a frilly white shrug. Her hair was pulled into a sleek bun, and her large white hoop earrings bounced with her every move. He wanted to snatch her close, free her curls and press his mouth on hers.

She made a point of opening the door wide so his secretary, Jan Kemp, had full view into his office.

His eyes were drawn to Shanna's plump lips. Moist and slick. He clamped his jaw to keep from groaning and was grateful for the desk concealing the bulge in his pants. She slipped into the chair across from him, placed her bag on the floor and folded her hands in her lap.

"Good morning," she said, tucking her legs beneath her. Her stoic expression was all business and would put off a less secure man.

"I see you made it home okay," he said, remembering those long legs wrapped around his back and struggling not to moan.

"Where there's a car service, there's a way." She looked at her watch. "I received your email that we needed to meet. I was hoping to get to my school this morning."

He pointed to a white bag on the small table in his office and asked, "Did you eat? I brought you an apple fritter from the little coffee shop by the pier."

Her brows raised. "You remembered?"

"I remember everything about you and our time together. You used to say there was never a wrong time of day to eat their apple fritters and there was nothing an apple fritter couldn't solve." Lynx had gotten up early that morning to get to the coffee shop so he could get the treat for her before they sold out. The coffee shop baked their goods fresh, and they used local ingredients and fruits whenever possible.

She eyed the bag, and he could see she was tempted to indulge, but she didn't move. "I was wrong. An apple fritter can't solve this scandal—or us."

Lynx stood, stalked over to his door and closed it.

"I'm sorry," he said, leaning against the door. "I snapped at you, and I shouldn't have. I have no excuse, so I hope you'll accept my heartfelt apology."

"Consider it forgotten," she said, flailing her hand.

Her dismissive wave irritated him. "So that's it?" he asked.

"Yes. What happened in North Carolina was a big mistake—one I don't plan on repeating." She jumped to her feet, her earrings swaying with the snap of her head.

"I understand, and I'll respect your wishes," he said, though her words had punctured his heart. Being with her felt right. Waking up next to her felt right. Nothing about their time together was a mistake. "For what it's worth, I want you to know I don't regret what happened. In fact, I'm honored you chose me."

She opened her mouth, and her eyes went wide. "Thank you for saying that. I just want us to move on, and I hope things won't be awkward between us going forward. We can just go back to the way things were before—uh, well, without the arguments, of course." She averted her eyes from his. He could hear her panting and could see her chest heaving.

Using every ounce of willpower he possessed, he kept his gaze on her face. Sweat beaded his brow, and he wondered if she could see the need written on his face.

Then she licked her lips.

Goodness. *Kill me now.*

Lynx remembered how those lips felt on his chest, on his back, and he closed his eyes for a second, uttering a quick silent prayer. There was no going back to the way things were before, but he wasn't going to argue. Tension swirled between them, thick and strong, refusing to be ignored. He fought the gripping urge to scoop her into his arms and partake of her right there in his office.

"Well?" she asked, coming into his space, perhaps unaware of her effect on him. Or maybe she was aware and she was driving him wild with need on purpose.

He strove to recall her last words but failed. All he could think about was her wearing that same perfume when they'd made love.

"What are you wearing?" he asked, hating how tortured he sounded.

She fidgeted with her shrug and whispered in a sultry tone, "Bombshell Intense. It's a mix of vanilla, peony and cherry, if I remember right."

He heard a guttural moan and realized he was the one who had made the sound. "That scent is perfect on you. It's driving me crazy."

"Oh. I see." She stepped back.

He reached out and wrapped his hand around her

arm. "I enjoyed you last week—all of you. I missed having you curled up next to me. It was only a few days, but I got used to you, and I don't know if I'll ever sleep the same again."

"We can't," she said, even though her eyes darkened. Desire raged in their depths, giving him hope.

"Tell me you don't want me anymore," he said, releasing her arm.

She lowered her head before slumping against him. "I can't do that." She ran her hands across his chest before pulling away and giving in to a safer urge. The paper bag crinkled as she opened it and took out the treat. Breaking it in half, she offered him a piece like she had done when they were teens. At least that hadn't changed. Lynx took it out of her hands; their brief contact sizzled. Shanna sank her teeth into the moist fritter, leaving telltale crumbs on the sides of her mouth.

"I know I said I'll respect your wishes, but I feel compelled to ask for another chance. I know I messed up, but I can do better." He used his finger to wipe off the remnants of the fritter and stuck his finger in his mouth.

Shanna's eyes followed his actions, but her lashes hid her thoughts from him. Touching his face, she changed the subject. "I get that you were upset about losing the chance to buy your grandfather's watch, but that does not excuse your behavior."

Lynx tossed the bag into the trash. "I know. My grandfather's watch was within reach, and it was a bitter disappointment to lose out to someone who is all about profit. I don't think that man understands or cares about the sentimental value it holds for me. All he sees are dollar signs."

"You think he's going to sell it?" she asked, cocking her head.

"I'm on the lookout, and I have several people keeping an eye out. If it comes back on the market, I'm getting that watch."

"Good."

A rap at the door made them put distance between them. He called out for Jan to enter once she'd identified herself. She had a printout in her hand.

"You both need to see this article I printed off the internet," she said, dropping the paper on his desk. "Your father called, saying he needs to meet with the both of you. It's urgent."

Jan's voice held a warning. His secretary wouldn't have interrupted if it wasn't a serious matter. Lynx already knew before looking at the paper he wasn't going to like what he saw.

"Thanks, Jan. I'll get in touch with him."

Shanna was already creeping toward the desk. As soon as Jan closed the door behind her, she picked up the paper. Her mouth dropped.

"No. No. No. This can't be happening," she said in horror, shaking the paper in her hand. "You know what this means? My reputation is now trashed. Toilet matter."

Lynx took the paper from her and read. Dread lined his stomach, the weight of cement blocks.

There was a picture of him and Shanna at the resort, white-water rafting, cuddled close together.

For the second time that morning, he found himself apologizing. "I'm sorry. I don't know how they found us or why they would print this." He raked a hand through his hair, worried about her—and himself.

"Because it's sensational." She grabbed the paper from him and waved it in the air. "It makes me look like I don't care. I'm happy and smiling, looking carefree, when my school is in the middle of a scandal." She shook her head. "I can't believe this is happening."

He sought to comfort her. "We can fix this."

"How?" she raged, placing a hand on her forehead before rubbing her eyes "We're displayed in full color for everyone to see."

"A picture doesn't prove anything. We are two associates having fun." Even as he spoke the words, he knew his response lacked merit. Their body language said it all. Her head was tilted, her neck exposed, and his mouth looked close to her ear. The picture showed they weren't just having a good time—they were into each other. Very much.

"On the contrary. It proves a lot. This is all over the world at this point. There is no fixing this." She broke into tears, the paper falling to the floor. "I'm sure your father is coming to tell me I no longer have a job."

She sank into the chair. Lynx rushed to her side and dropped to his knees.

"I don't think that's why he's here. And even if it is, we need to come up with a better solution."

"What *solution*? What can we say? I shouldn't have gone to North Carolina with you. That was a stupid move that I didn't think through. Now I'm in an even bigger scandal than before. Okay, I'm exaggerating. Maybe the word I'm looking for is *sensational*." She placed her head in her hands. "Ugh. Being with you is going to ruin me."

Her regret pierced his soul, tearing him apart in ways he couldn't verbalize. He felt like someone had taken a hammer and jammed a nail into his heart.

Lynx stood. Her words echoed in his mind, taunting him, jeering at him. His heart couldn't hold up under the impact of the despondency etched on her beautiful face. Knowing he was responsible, even indirectly, crushed him to the core.

Shattered, he staggered back to his desk; the truth a burden. He didn't know how he was going to fix this, but he would.

He wouldn't rest until he had a solution.

He didn't know the words to describe the tumultuous emotions reeling within him, but he knew he would do whatever it took to see her smile.

Chapter Twenty-Two

Shanna had no defense, but she spent the entire ten minutes until Patrick arrived trying to think of one.

The superintendent stormed into Lynx's office. "Give me one good reason why I shouldn't recommend both your resignations," he said, not bothering with a greeting, holding a copy of the online article in his hand. His eyes blazed.

She shrank into her seat and shook her head. "I don't have one."

Not one she could voice aloud, anyway.

He turned to Lynx, who came forward to stand next to her. "What do you have to say for yourself? Life is about timing and discretion, especially with the public feeding on us like wolves. I would think you would know better."

"We're allowed to have a private life," Lynx said in a steely tone. "What happens between me and Shanna off the clock is no one's business. Not even yours."

They stood before her, huffing with the fury of avenging angels. Neither looked like they would give an edge or back down. Shanna hated seeing father and son square off because of her. She stood and placed a hand on Lynx's arm, appreciating the feel of his muscular biceps. The memory of those same arms wrapped around her teased her mind.

"I'm sorry, Patrick," she said, fighting off the wave of desire rocking her body. "We weren't thinking."

"It's obvious," he sputtered, pushing his glasses up the bridge of his nose, visibly making an effort to calm down. "Because of this, I can't reassign you to work with Lynx. I'm going to have to put you on administrative leave. And frankly, I can't guarantee you'll be able to return."

She gasped, stepping away from Lynx. Her body quivered as the impact of the superintendent's words swept through her system. "Love Creek is my home. I love my job. I need to know I'll have a place here when my name is cleared—and it *will* be cleared."

"You spit on that job when you went gallivanting with my son at some resort. Public opinion drives decisions."

"We didn't do it on purpose," she said. *Gallivanting.* She didn't like the connotation behind that archaic word choice.

"My private life is not up for public debate," Lynx said, folding his arms, stretching the blue polo shirt he was wearing. A muscle under his left eye ticked, and he looked ready to explode.

"It is when you consort with the woman who's the face of a high-profile scandal," his father snapped, waving the article inches away from Lynx's face. He took out his handkerchief and wiped his face. His chest heaved, and Shanna worried that Patrick would give himself a stroke if he didn't calm down.

Consort. Another ancient, seedy word. She swallowed the bitter taste of being perceived as a loose woman. A pariah. A woman stained with the scarlet letter of scandal. She bit her lower lip to keep from breaking down.

Lynx brushed his hair out of his face. "Stop talking to Shanna as if she's a stranger to you. You know her. I would appreciate it if you speak to her with the respect she deserves."

Patrick raised a brow. "This is from the man who told me point-blank you couldn't vouch for her character."

Shanna touched her stomach. Hearing how Lynx perceived her from someone else hurt her more than she would ever admit. She knew he didn't trust her, but she didn't know he had shared those views with someone else—particularly her boss. On the other hand, his father was pretty shady, outing his son's confidence in that manner. Her respect for the superintendent cooled a few degrees.

She swung her eyes to Lynx, knowing her face

depicted her pain at that revelation and needing him to see it.

Lynx looked chagrined, but he rose to her defense. "Whatever I said was before I got to know her better this past week. I misjudged her, and I'm prepared to stand by and defend her integrity—and you should as well."

The superintendent looked properly chastised. His shoulders slumped, and he lowered his voice several octaves. "My son is right. I'm sorry, Shanna. I overreacted. I've been under enormous pressure, and seeing my son's face in the paper pushed me over the edge. He's worked so hard to get where he is—you both have, actually. So there's no justifiable excuse for my unprofessional behavior, and for that, I do apologize." He gave her a fatherly pat on the hand. "I value you as an employee, and you've been an asset to our district."

"I understand," Shanna said, her respect reinstated. Somewhat. "You're a father trying to protect your son." She could appreciate that.

"I don't need protecting." Lynx placed an arm around her shoulder and brought her close.

Patrick's shrewd eyes zoned in on them.

His gesture left no doubt that their relationship—if that's what one could call it—had shifted into the personal. She stiffened and shifted, hoping he would break the physical contact, but he gave her shoulder a squeeze.

"Nevertheless, we will need to prepare a public statement. I'll have Susan work on it. In the meantime, I suggest you two keep your distance from each other until the investigation has been completed." In other words, he didn't want his son's stellar reputation sullied by keeping her company.

"That's not going to happen," Lynx growled, bringing her closer to him.

Shanna didn't understand why Lynx seemed determined to challenge his father. He could do that because he had nothing to lose. But she did, and she was going to cooperate as long as the request was made within reason. Patrick's request made sense.

"We can do that, sir. Do you have any word on the progress so far?"

He wiped his brow. "I'm not at liberty to say as yet—but I *will* say things are looking up. We will be wrapping up your inquiry in another week or two."

Shanna released a plume of air. Like a vine circling a fence, she clung to the small degree of hope his words provided.

"Your administrative leave starts now," he said to her, then addressed Lynx. "If you truly want to be the next superintendent of Love Creek, son, you're going to have to make unfavorable decisions at times. Because you serve everyone. The community, the staff, the children—everyone."

Shanna felt a pang knowing she would never hold that role. Her name was synonymous with scandal. A scandal that had been a guillotine to her career in education. Even if—no, when—she was cleared, the damage was already done. She fought back tears. It stung. Knowing she had almost crossed the finish line and through no fault of her own, she had been tripped in the race. She couldn't even limp her way to victory. Neither could she concede defeat. She just didn't know what to do.

Lynx cleared his throat. In a much calmer tone, he asked, "What if there was another solution?"

She whipped her head Lynx's way to see his mind churning. Her stomach clenched. Somehow, she knew she wouldn't like what he was about to say.

"What if Shanna and I announced we're getting married?" he asked, stuffing his hands in his pants pockets.

"How is that fixing the issue?" his father asked.

"Wh—what?" she said, placing a hand on her chest. Her breath caught. She pictured herself dressed in that lace gown she had seen in North Carolina and a simple veil, carrying a small bouquet of flowers. With her sister walking next to her, she would saunter down the aisle to meet Lynx. Dressed in his black tux, he would be all smiles, his eyes filled with...love?

She hoped.

But Lynx's next words trampled that vision out of her mind.

He paced the room. "That's how we fix this. We tell everyone we've been dating and went away to celebrate our engagement. Then, once this is all settled, we can say we've parted ways. Irreconcilable differences. It's a win-win situation."

Not for her, it wasn't.

She must have been mistaken or in need of hearing aids. A fake engagement. His proposal—no pun intended—was ridiculous. And insulting. She shook her head. That was his remedy for this chaos that was now her life? Even his father's face bore an expression of horror. Before Patrick could utter a word, Shanna jumped in.

"A fake engagement would reek of desperation and add fuel to the speculation that I'm receiving preferential treatment," she said, her anger building.

Lynx stopped. It was obvious he hadn't considered that.

"I imagine you're trying to be a hero. I'm not helpless or in need of rescue. The fact that you would suggest something of that magnitude without asking me is evidence of your arrogance."

The fact that she had a moment where she'd dared to dream it was for real was sorry. Disappointment was a bitter pill. Rather than swallow it, she cloaked herself with pride.

"I was trying to help," he said, holding out a hand.

"Is that what you think you were doing?" she asked, raising a brow. "Do me a favor. Don't. Just don't." She tapped her feet. Not once since she was a girl daydreaming of marriage had she imagined she would receive her first proposal in this manner and under these circumstances. Lynx had tossed out the terms with a glibness that rankled and then in the same breath announced their demise.

"Enough," Patrick said, looking between them. "You both will report to Human Resources and complete a consensual relationship disclosure. Then we will release the statement announcing Shanna's administrative leave."

She gave a jerky nod. "How long will I be punished for something I didn't do?"

"I envision three months or so. The investigators have a lot of children and staff to question, and most people are still on vacation."

"So even if I'm cleared, I wouldn't be allowed to return to work until all this is over?" She hated to ask, but she had to. "Will this be paid administrative leave?"

"I don't think the board will agree to that," he said, his tone sympathetic.

So months without an income. She had savings and some minor investments, but that wouldn't last. She swallowed. Maybe she should put her mother's house up for sale. The thought of that squeezed her heart—but it was a seller's market.

"Can't you offer her a position in the district office?" Lynx asked. "She could manage transportation or handle discipline and expulsions."

Again, Lynx spoke for her without asking her opinion. However, since this suggestion had merit, she held her tongue. For now.

Patrick rubbed his chin. "Let me speak with the board. I'll get back to you on that." He gave Lynx a meaningful stare. "We will talk, son."

Once Patrick had departed the room, Shanna confronted Lynx. "Did I say I wanted to do busywork?"

He shook his head. "I don't get you. Why do you find it hard to accept my help? I care about your welfare. You might not like dealing with angry parents or the bus driver deficit, but you'll have an income. It's like you're disagreeing for the sole purpose of arguing with me."

"You don't get it," she said, shaking her head. "I'm not saying it isn't a good strategy, but this is about respecting me enough to ask my opinion."

She could see when her words sank in.

"I see," he said, shoulders deflated. "I'm sorry I wasn't considerate of your feelings. Just know my intentions were pure, though my execution sucked."

"Speaking of which. Announcing our engagement?" She placed a hand on her hip. "That was audacious. Was I supposed to go along like a puppet on a string?" Her heart thumped against her chest, anticipating his answer. She was surprised to know how much his next words mattered to her.

He didn't answer the question. Instead, he asked, hurt evident in his tone and sadness reflected in his blue eyes, "Would it have been so awful to claim me as your fiancé?"

Chapter Twenty-Three

Lynx waited with bated breath for Shanna to respond. He had made a rash offer, but her rejection of him hurt. She hadn't even taken the time to think about it before snapping at him.

Shanna massaged her temples. "How do you expect me to answer you with any level of seriousness when what you were proposing wasn't even real?"

"It would have been real." And part of him would have welcomed it. Anticipated having her by his side. Claiming her as his own. It would have been the two of them standing against the masses.

"For a short time," she scoffed, playing with her shrug. She grabbed her bag, a silent code she was done with this conversation.

He decided to let the matter rest because he was

obviously doing a poor job of communicating his feelings. His heart ached in silence.

"Let's just get to HR and complete the forms," she said, striding toward the door.

He followed her. "We can go together, if you'd like." He tensed while she mulled it over.

"The media could be there, waiting for us," she said.

He dared to reach for her hand. "I'm not ashamed to be seen with you."

Moments later, he helped her get settled in his car. Lynx wished she had responded with something like, "I'm not ashamed of you, either." But all he had gotten was a small nod of agreement before she continued out to the parking lot.

He put on the radio for the ten-minute ride. Shanna spent most of the time rubbing her legs and looking out the window. He wanted to ask her to share what was on her mind but didn't want to be rebuffed. He sighed, hating how they were no longer in sync. Still, he was glad to have more time in her presence, no matter the reason.

Forty minutes later, they were back outside the high school. He could see Shanna fighting to regain her control. She had a hand on the door handle but had yet to open the door. The HR rep, who had returned from vacation, had handed her the official letter placing her on leave, stating the board hadn't wanted to reassign her to a desk job. At least it wasn't his father handling it this time.

Lynx had clenched his jaw to keep from yelling,

applauding Shanna's restraint. She had been gracious and courteous, which made her even more beautiful to him. Only when they returned to his car had the tears trekked down her face. Her sniffles chopped at his heart. He didn't know what to say, so he opted for simplicity.

Lynx received a text from his father, asking him to stop by the house later. He answered, stating he would, before returning his attention to the woman in his car.

"I'm sorry, Shanna," he said.

She nodded. "I don't know who I am without my job."

"You're still you. Wonderful. Amazing. Talented. Your career doesn't define who you are. You're more than that. This will pass, and you'll be stronger than you were before."

"Do you really think so?" she asked in a small voice filled with doubt.

"Yes. With one hundred percent certainty."

With a nod, she exited the car. She took rapid steps, wiping her face every now and then. Lynx knew she didn't believe him. He also knew he couldn't let her leave in that state. He opened the door and got out. His words hadn't reached her, but maybe his actions would. Heedless of the fact they were in the school parking lot and the media might be following them, Lynx rushed after her. But he was too late. She was already in her vehicle and backing out. He followed her home, pulling into her drive-way behind her.

"I just want to go inside, Lynx," she called out to him after rolling down her window. Everything about her tone said she didn't want company, but her eyes communicated to his heart.

He parked, got out of his car and held out his hands. "Come to me."

"That would not be the wisest move. I don't want to chance having our faces plastered all over the news."

"I'm not moving. There's nothing wrong with providing comfort to a friend."

She opened the SUV door, leaving it wide open, and stomped up to him. The moment she was in his arms, she broke into tears. She cried and cried, leaning into him as she released her tears. He reached around her waist, resting his arms around her bottom, squeezing her close. He rocked her until she calmed. Without a word, she pulled out of his arms and rubbed at the wet spot on his shirt; then she turned off her SUV, leaned inside to get her purse and walked up to her front door.

"I'm coming inside." He spoke the words with authority, but it was all a bluff. He prayed she wouldn't say no. That two-letter word had power, and as a man, he would respect that. A few beats passed where she seemed to be in a debate with herself.

Then she shrugged.

She hadn't denied him entrance.

A good sign.

Lynx stepped past the threshold of her private domain for the first time. Normally, he would take in his surroundings, but he only had eyes for Shanna, and his mind registered that they were alone. She dropped her bag to the floor and twisted around to face him.

"Why are you here?" she asked, shaking her head. "Aren't you worried about being us being here together, after everything?"

"We have declared our relationship to the people who need to know and when it comes to you, there's nowhere else for me to be."

Her face softened. "Just when I think…" She sighed. "And then you go and say something like that…" She flailed her hands. "I'm incoherent because I don't know what to say or do with you right now. One minute, you're demanding and I want to cuss you out. And the next, you're sweet and I want to—" She stopped and pursed her lips. "What am I going to do with you?"

So many words spun through his mind, but they would have come off as a line. So Lynx said nothing. He would let her take the lead, pull the strings. Especially since she had accused him of being a puppet master. This time, she was in charge.

She breathed out. "My sister's gone for the day…" She added that Yanni had driven out to the outlets to do some shopping and would be return the following evening.

His heart skipped a beat. The air tensed. He got her implication, but a man should never jump to conclusions.

Shanna loosened her bun, and her hair fell to her

shoulders in waves. Lynx wanted to run his fingers through the strands, massage her neck and plant soft kisses on her face—communicate all he had to say without words. He felt a burning and a yearning for her with an intensity that surprised him. He wanted to cross the distance and give into his needs, but Lynx summoned his inner will to stand in place. To wait.

Fully dressed, he felt vulnerable.

Open.

She tossed her wedges, took off her white jacket, never taking her eyes off him. He swallowed, warning himself not to read into her actions. But his eyes feasted on her exposed shoulders. His tongue ached to taste her beautiful brown skin.

Shanna pivoted and strutted toward a room he figured must be her bedroom. She stopped at the door. Then she turned and gave him a provocative look. "I'm going to take a shower. Are you coming?" There was no mistaking that invitation. He took in her darkened eyes and her slightly parted begging-to-be-kissed lips, and his mouth went dry.

Then he sprang into action.

Lynx called the school to speak to his secretary, Jan, trying not to groan when Shanna shimmied out of her jumper, placing a hand on the strap of her bra. Desire slammed into him. He sucked in a huge breath of oxygen and addressed Jan. "I'm taking the rest of the day off," he said in a rush before ending the call. After dropping the phone to the floor, he tugged off his shoes, jumped out of his pants and skittered behind Shanna as eager as a hungry puppy about to be fed.

Chapter Twenty-Four

Shanna felt sexy, desirable, wanted—and it was all because of the man snoring beside her. After squeezing together in the small shower, they had made love, eaten and made love again. It was early afternoon, and the sun was out. She could hear the voices of her neighbor's children playing by the side of her house. Their mother must have put out the sprinkler to cool them off. She giggled at their squeals of delight, placing a hand on her stomach. One day, she hoped to be a mother.

She experienced a momentary panic, remembering Lynx hadn't worn a condom the first time they had made love. This time, however, he had been prepared. She doubted she had anything to worry about.

Snuggling close to him, she appreciated his warm,

chiseled body. He wrapped her in his arms. Lying there with their bodies spooning together, she admitted the answer to Lynx's question: it wouldn't be awful to claim him as her fiancé.

In fact, it would be wonderful.

Heart-happy wonderful.

Which was why she couldn't accept his pretend offer. Because for one of them—meaning her—it wouldn't be a pretense. It would be realer than real.

She reached for her phone and searched social media to see if their picture was circulating online. It was. She observed the contrast of his white skin against her brown. Love Creek had a lot of interracial couples, but that didn't mean racism didn't exist—inside and out of the town. Below their photo, people commented, calling her and Lynx ugly names and sellouts. She refused to get angry. Tossing the phone onto the nightstand, she acknowledged that she would've been surprised if no one had mentioned their race.

Sad state of the world.

At the end of the day, these cowards did nothing to add to her life. They were the same hypocrites who would smile in her face while holding the knife to puncture her lungs.

A strong urge to pee made her slip out of bed and traipse across the room toward the bathroom. She caught a glance of herself in the mirror and gasped. Her swollen lips, flushed face and wild hair were a testament to how she'd spent her day.

When she was finished relieving herself, she

washed her hands and dried them on a white towel with red roses. Worn and frayed at the edges, though clean, it had to be at least ten years old. Shanna stilled. That was a long time. She scanned the room, noting the broken tiles with stained grout, the chipped tub and the water-soaked sink.

Her forced vacation might be the ideal time to get some of these tasks done. She brushed her teeth and rinsed with Listerine.

Peering around the corner to see if Lynx was still sleeping, Shanna felt embarrassment crawl up her spine. She didn't know what he would think of her home. And she shouldn't care, she told herself.

Shanna opened her chest of drawers and chose a pair of plaid shorts with a blue tank she had bought on sale from Old Navy. Then she went into her kitchen to open and close the cupboards, seeing if anything spoke to her stomach. She snapped her fingers, remembering she had placed a package of ground turkey inside the fridge to cook tacos. Opening the cupboard to the right of the stove, she pulled out a packet of taco seasoning; then she bent over to get a pan from under the sink.

A pair of strong hands grabbed her butt, and she yelped.

"You scared the life out of me," she said, straightening.

"I didn't mean to alarm you, but your butt in the air was begging to be touched." Lynx pecked her on the lips. His breath smelled minty, and he had put on his black boxer briefs. "What are you doing?"

"I'm getting ready to make tacos."

He nodded. "That's what's up." Rubbing his hands together, he asked, "What do you need me to do?"

She poured some water from the gallon jug— she never used Florida's tap water—into the electric kettle and pressed the lever to turn it on. It was one of the few modern amenities Yanni had insisted she buy.

"If you could dice the tomatoes and cut up the avocados, that would be great. They're in the vegetable drawer. Oh, and can you grab the bag of shredded lettuce?"

"All right. I'll be right back." He returned seconds later, wearing his polo shirt and now wrinkled pants.

Lynx washed his hands, gathered the items and went to work. She emptied the turkey in the pan and turned on the one of two burners that still worked. She used a serving fork to mash the turkey. Once it was finished cooking, she drained it, then poured in the taco seasoning and hot water, which would help make the sauce.

"I'm all done," Lynx said. He had everything chopped in a neat pile on the chopping board.

"Perfect. Now all I need is the taco boats and a can of black beans." She told him where to find them and handed Lynx a hand-operated can opener. He fumbled with the older contraption until he was able to open the can of beans.

They set everything up on the small dinette table with rickety chairs, but Lynx didn't complain. He devoured two tacos and was working on a third when Shanna got out a bottle of raspberry lemonade.

"These are delicious," he said, biting into the boat. Some of the juice ran down his chin, heading toward his shirt.

She couldn't have that. She put down her boat and leaned over the table and licked the sauce. He groaned.

They made eye contact.

Lynx raked his fingers in her hair and tilted her head back before leaning over to kiss her. His tongue explored the cavern of her mouth with a thoroughness that left her winded and wet. Lynx scooped her into his arms.

She protested. "I'm too heavy to lift. I don't want you to hurt yourself."

He chuckled and walked toward the bedroom. When he rested her on the bed, he wasn't out of breath. What a turn-on.

"Get on your back."

Lynx complied with a quickness that made her laugh. She straddled him. "Do you know why they call this position the female superior?"

He shook his head. "No. Why?"

She smiled. "I'm about to show you."

Chapter Twenty-Five

Lynx dragged himself out of Shanna's house a couple of hours later, tired and satisfied. He and Shanna had done some things that couldn't be repeated but would never be forgotten. The only reason why he was leaving was because he had to see his father. He drove home, showered and dressed, and arrived at his parents' home at about six o'clock.

He used his key to let himself in and made his way to the family room, fighting back his guilt. He should have been coming in with Pop's watch. He shrugged off the disappointment and walked past the kitchen. Without his brothers around, the house seemed vacuous and large. As expected, his father was in the family room, watching *Family Feud* with Steve Harvey as host. There was a huge glass of Pepsi in his cup holder, and Patrick's snack of choice, a Ziploc bag of granola, was on the seat next to him. Most of the time, his parents kept a healthy diet, but Patrick refused to give up his one vice: Pepsi Cola. He kept cases in the garage.

"They've gotten a little raunchy since he took over the show," Patrick said, stretching out on the recliner.

"They're trying to appeal to a younger crowd," Lynx said, looking at the screen. "You have to admit Steve's tie game is sharp, though."

His mother came into the room and kissed him on the cheek. "Are you hungry?" she asked. "I made pot roast."

"I'm stuffed," he said, patting his stomach.

"Do you want me to pack you a container?" she offered.

He nodded. "Thanks, Mom." He almost never left his parents' house without being fed.

She left the room. Lynx was surprised she hadn't mentioned the newspaper article. Maybe his father had told her not to bring it up.

His father held the remote toward the television to turn it off; then he pierced Lynx with a gaze. Lynx squared his shoulders. From the look on his father's face, whatever he had to say to Lynx was serious.

"What's going on with you and Shanna?" he asked in a low voice.

"What do you mean?" Lynx asked, settling onto the couch.

Patrick cleared his throat and pushed his glasses up his face. "Your mother and I agreed years ago that once you boys got to a certain age, we wouldn't interfere in your relationships. We want all our sons to find their love match organically. The only time we've ever gotten involved was if we were asked for advice. And given all of your success, we've never had to step into your affairs."

Lynx twiddled his thumbs. This felt like the beginning of the hamburger method of constructive criticism—compliment-criticism-compliment. It was a tool he practiced himself when conferencing with parents and teachers.

"You've accomplished so much at a young age. You're at the right place to take my seat when I retire."

Compliment.

"However, your actions of late with Shanna have been way past questionable. She's a remarkable woman, but considering the circumstances, a spontaneous getaway was not a wise move, career wise."

Criticism.

"We have a population of 15,000 in the town, and you have your choice of women. You're one of our town's most eligible bachelors. Perhaps you need to cast your net a little wider."

Compliment. Sort of.

Patrick took a sip of Pepsi and gave Lynx a pointed glare.

Lynx scooted to the edge of the seat. "Dad, I can't believe you just hamburgered me."

"Did it work?"

He chuckled. At least his father hadn't denied it. "She's special."

"If you think so, you shouldn't toy with her feelings. She's going through a rough patch. Things might get worse before they get better."

He narrowed his eyes. "What makes you think I'm toying with her? You raised me right."

"Give her up, son," Patrick urged, getting to his feet. Those four words landed like boulders in his stomach. He felt like he'd been tossed into the water and was now sinking to the bottom.

"Sever all ties until this scandal blows over. Then you can date a porcupine, and I wouldn't care."

Don't see her. Don't touch her.

That was like asking him not to breathe. Or eat. Or sleep.

No.

Lynx stood and met his father's gaze head-on. "That's not an option."

"The board has you on a pedestal. I don't want you shaking their faith in you."

"Are you threatening me with the job if I don't do as you say?" he asked through gritted teeth.

Patrick didn't blink or back down.

Tanya came into the room and stood between them, facing Lynx. "Your father is making a mess out of this. He likes Shanna well enough. She's ambitious. She has drive, but the issue is timing. This isn't the right time. Maybe you should wait." She tapped his shoulder.

Trust his mother to sum up the situation in under five seconds.

"I can't wait, and I don't want to," Lynx said. Even being here with them, he missed Shanna already. And it had only been a little past an hour. "For all you and Mom went through to be together, I'm shocked to hear you tell me to back off." He jutted his chin toward his father. "You told us you used to sit outside Mom's house for hours—*hours*—just to drive her to school, which was a couple of blocks away from her home." Then he faced his mother. "Your parents wanted you to marry Theodore Morris, but you chose Dad. You told me there's a sizzle—an electricity that never diminishes—when you're with Dad." He held his mother's hand. "Well, over the past week, that's how I feel when I'm with Shanna. We laugh, we argue and we…" He paused. No point in divulging too much information. "I feel a crackle when I'm in her presence. I feel like I'm ten times the man I am just because I'm with her."

Lynx stopped. He knew his face had reddened under his passionate outburst. He sounded like a man who had it bad, and he was slightly embarrassed. But he had meant every word.

Tanya touched her chest, her eyes wide and bright. "Are you in love with Shanna?"

Her question sucker punched him. In the gut. In his heart.

"It's too soon," his father growled.

"You knew within hours of meeting me," Tanya pointed out.

Lynx tuned out his parents' good-natured bickering and strolled over to the other end of the room. There was a picture of him from high school. He had taken up wrestling and won first prize in the team competition. In the photo, Lynx held up the medal with a smile stretched across his face. It was the first time he had won anything. He pointed to the picture. "Do you remember how I wore this medal everywhere for months? I slept in it. I even wore it in the shower. Everybody I met heard about that medal."

Patrick chuckled. "We couldn't get you to take that thing off."

He nodded. "That's how I feel about Shanna. I want to take her everywhere with me, and I want to shout to the entire world and tell them how amazing she is. She's always been fine, but I'm kicking myself for not seeing her true essence sooner. But now that I've seen her, there's no unseeing her for me." He looked at his father when he said those words.

Tanya's mouth hung open. She uttered an eloquent, "Oh." She ambled over to join his side and held out a hand. "If that's how you feel about Shanna, son, don't let her go. I'm in your corner, both literally and figuratively."

His mother was such a romantic. He would have laughed, but he realized that was exactly what *he* had become too.

"Have you told her?" his father asked, then took a huge gulp of his Pepsi.

Lynx shook his head. "I didn't realize her effect on me until just now."

"Shanna is a way better match than the Crane," his mother chimed in, using the nickname his brothers had for Irene.

"How's Irene handling the article? I can't see her being all right with this," Patrick asked.

He felt an unease rise within him. "But we're broken up," he said.

Tanya waved a hand. "And like I told him when he first told me, good riddance. She was all wrong for him. Bland. Selfish."

"She wasn't wrapped too tight." His father wagged a finger. "Mark my words—that girl will make trouble just for trouble's sake."

Patrick's prediction chilled him to the core. A picture of Shanna and Lynx together was all over social media and the news. It was odd that Irene hadn't reached out to wail about how he had done her wrong. Never mind that she had ended things or had been sleeping around. She wouldn't see it that way.

But their last encounter had been final. There was no coming back from him putting her out of his house. No, he decided—he had cut that cord for good. He wouldn't waste another minute thinking about Irene. He needed to focus on what really mattered.

Patrick turned up the television, signaling that the conversation was over. His mother went on about planning a wedding, ignoring Lynx's attempts at telling her to slow down. She left the room, saying she was going to research wedding sites.

"What's going on with Shanna's investigation?"

he asked. "We need to get her name cleared because she didn't do this."

"I know she didn't," Patrick said.

He slinked onto the couch. "Then why did you put her on leave?" he asked, anger creeping into his tone.

"Because there may be more to this scandal than we realized," he said, pressing the button to lower the volume. "We received a threat, and the police are investigating."

Lynx's heart thumped. "What kind of a threat? Why didn't you tell me? Is Shanna in danger?" He fired off the questions in one breath.

"Easy now," his father said. "All will be well— in due time."

"I can't take it easy," he said, standing. "I've got to tell Shanna."

"You will do no such thing," Patrick said in a steely voice. "I'm talking as your boss."

"If this were Mom, what would you do?"

"It isn't your mother, and I would like to think I'd follow what law enforcement is telling me to do." His voice held a warning tone.

Lynx pursed his lips, knowing his father wasn't being honest. He folded his arms. "Tell me."

Patrick drained his Pepsi. "Someone hacked into Shanna's work email. We know it isn't her because it was a different IP address. Whoever this is has been tracking her and even took that picture of the two of you. This person accused Shanna of being the mastermind behind the cheating and demanded if she didn't pay, they would take care of her."

A money-hungry reporter was one thing. A psycho with purpose was another.

Thus, the real reason his father had placed her on leave. Lynx should have known something was up because that behavior had been outside Patrick's character. His father had no qualms fighting the board when he wanted something done.

Lynx shot to his feet. "What if I didn't bring up the case just now? Would you have told me?" he roared. "Shanna's life might be in danger. She deserves to know what's going on. This is her life we're talking about."

"You'll keep quiet. You can't tip her off. The cops have a hunch, and they're closing in on the perpetrator. Just give it a few days."

"Give me one good reason why I should keep silent and put Shanna in jeopardy? I'm getting out of here." He strode out of the room, intending to head home to pack a bag and—no. He'd convince Shanna to come home with him. He had an advanced security system. She would be safe with him.

Patrick caught up to him and grabbed his arm, his eyes ablaze. "I'll make it easy for you to keep your mouth shut. You forget this is a small town. I've known most of the board members since they were in Pampers. They respect me. They listen to me. Tell her, and you can kiss the superintendent job goodbye."

Chapter Twenty-Six

"Mom is going to be so glad to see you," Shanna said to Yanni. They stood huddled by the well-tended potted bamboo plant outside their mother's room at the nursing home. She had persuaded her sister to pay Bernice a visit before going back to school. Yanni had received word she had been accepted for a teaching position, and they were going out to celebrate after their visit.

The school district had released the statement earlier in the day. Shanna had watched it on the news. So many people had praised the district's decision to demote her, not caring how she would survive. Thank goodness Lynx had been there to comfort her.

The fact that Yanni hadn't mentioned her administrative leave, meant Yanni hadn't caught the news and Shanna wasn't going to enlighten her. Ruin the mood. Besides, she didn't want Yanni to worry.

Shanna slung an arm over her sister's shoulders. "You have to share your good news with Mom. She'll be so proud of you."

"If she remembers me," Yanni said.

She opened the door, and they went inside. Their mother sat on her bed, studying a picture. Yanni and Shanna approached with caution, trying to ascertain her mood. Bernice lifted her head and smiled. "Girls!" She stood, placed the picture on the nightstand and held out her hands. "I'm so glad you came to see me."

Shanna's stomach muscles relaxed. She gestured to Yanni to go first, because there was no telling how long Bernice would be present. It could be hours. Or mere minutes. Yanni needed to soak in this moment for as long as it lasted.

Yanni emitted a sigh of relief and rushed to hug their mother. "I miss you, Mom. I'm so glad you're you today." Her shoulders shook, and she began to sob.

"Silly girl. Who else would I be?" Bernice rocked her, patting her on the back. "How's school going?"

"I'm almost finished with my master's, and I got a teaching job at the university. I'll have two undergrad classes," Yanni said, the words rushing out. Shanna understood why and tried to hold in her tears.

"Shanna's dating a white man," Yanni continued.

Bernice chuckled. "Hush, now. You always loved telling your sister's business."

"Yep," Shanna said, walking forward to kiss her mother on the cheek. "She was always getting me in trouble, and every time, I'd say that's the last time I confide in her."

"Until the next time," Yanni said, holding their mother's hand in a death grip.

The women shared in the laugh—a normal laugh between a mother and her children. Yanni's and Shanna's eyes met. Shanna led her mother back to the bed, and they both sat on either side of her. Yanni's face was shining, and Shanna knew hers was as well. She was so glad she had visited today.

A text alert came in from Lynx, but Shanna didn't want to use up precious time with her mother talking to him. She would answer him later.

"Mom, you know what? Shanna bought a SUV. I told her to get it because you know how hard she works, and she totally deserved it. I kept telling her the principal needs to arrive to work in style."

Bernice touched Shanna's cheek. "I'm so proud of you." She cocked her head. "So tell me about your beau."

"He's white, and he's hot," Yanni blurted out.

"Yanni, give your sister a chance to get a word in. I'm not going anywhere. You'll get your chance."

Shanna's heart twisted. If only Bernice knew the truth. That she would leave them soon. It wasn't a matter of *if* but *when*. She injected a light tone and answered her mom. "Yanni's talking about Lynx. You remember him. We went to school together."

Bernice nodded, but Shanna knew her mother didn't recall. He wasn't in her long-term memory.

"Yeah. They used to hate each other, and now he's got her all googly-eyed," Yanni said.

"Whatever," Shanna said, rolling her eyes. Yanni was right. He did have her googly-eyed, contorting her in all sorts of shapes and positions. *Whew.* She had better take up yoga because flexibility and stamina were needed. An adventurous lover who was also a compassionate man was a potent combination.

Bernice looked at Yanni. "What about you? Have you met someone?"

Yanni shook her head. "No way. I ain't got time for all that. A relationship is too much for me to handle right now. I have to focus on my studies." Shanna chuckled at Yanni's horror. She made a relationship sound like a disease, something to avoid.

Bernice looked away, zoning out—a sign she was slipping away. Shanna squeezed her mother's hand, refusing to panic. There was something she needed to know before Bernice retreated into her world. "Mom, are you happy here? Are they treating you all right in here?"

"Yes, love," she said, looking at Shanna with a steady gaze. "The food needs some salt and pepper, but I'm learning to live with that. Don't worry about me. I'm good."

"Hold on, Mom," Shanna said. Shanna whispered to her sister. "Hug her, now."

Yanni hugged her mother, once again teary-eyed. "Don't go, Mom," she said in a small voice.

"Hmm." Bernice pointed to the picture on the wall and asked, "Who are those people?"

Tears pricked Shanna's eyes. "That's you, me and Yanni, Mom." She answered the question, though she knew her response wouldn't mean anything. "You made us take that picture together right after your diagnosis. You made me promise to hang it over your bed once you moved here," she said, keeping the response informative so Bernice wouldn't become agitated. She rose from the bed, and Yanni followed her.

"'Mom?" Bernice shuddered. "Who are you? Why are you here?" Her lips quivered as she looked between them.

"You're safe with us," Shanna said, reaching for one of the teddy bears. "How about you hold this so you're not afraid?"

Bernice nodded and clutched the stuffed animal close.

Yanni covered her face in her hands. "She's gone. Oh God."

"Don't focus on that and torture yourself. Think about the good conversation we just had. I'll meet you in the car," Shanna said. Her sister ran from the room. She understood how Yanni felt. Bernice was present in body only. Each time she left their world, it was like having a loved one die and die again. It chipped away at her faith. Shanna lived for those moments of clarity—signs Bernice was very much alive and present. She never remembered to hit the record button on her cell phone, though.

"Mom?" she asked once they were alone.

"I'm not your mom!" Bernice screamed. "I don't know who you are, but you'd better get out of here before I call the police."

"It's all right." Shanna's heart raced. She reached over to try to calm her mother, but Bernice shrugged her off.

Jumping to her feet, Bernice ran out of the room and into the hallway. "Help me! Help me, please!" she yelled.

Shanna scurried behind her as the aides scampered to flank Bernice.

"It's all right, Bernice," one of them said.

"Get me out of here," Bernice said, shaking her head. Her face held fear. Shanna told herself not to take it personally, but the terror etched on her mom's face slashed at her heart. She knew the nurse would have to give Bernice a sedative if they couldn't calm her.

"You should go," another aide said. "We'll get her settled. Don't worry."

With a shaky nod, Shanna raced out of the building. She rushed past a man she thought she knew, but she was too caught up in her feelings to be sure. Once she stepped outside, she wiped her face and drew in deep breaths. Every time Bernice became rational, Shanna told herself not to get hopeful, but she did. Bernice acted so…normal. It was easy to be lulled into thinking it would last.

She composed herself and rejoined Yanni in the car. Her sister's eyes were puffy, and she had put on her AirPods, a silent indication that she didn't want to talk.

Without a word, Shanna started the car.

"I want to go home," Yanni said.

"We are going to celebrate," Shanna said, enunciating each word. "You were chosen out of two hundred applicants. Jobs aren't easy to get in these times. That calls for a celebration."

"I don't feel like it."

"Doesn't matter. We're doing this."

Her sister slumped in her seat, leaning close to the door. Shanna ignored her silent tantrum, praying Yanni wouldn't sulk for long.

"I hate that you're making me do this when Mom is…" Yanni trailed off, sniffling.

Shanna softened, but she continued driving toward the restaurant. "It's what Mom would have wanted. You can't argue with that."

Yanni's mood lifted during their meal at Outback Steakhouse. She flirted with their server, Daniel, and accepted his number. Her sister agreed to meet up with him once his shift ended, rattling off their address without hesitation. Shanna uttered a word of caution, but Yanni shrugged her off, telling her to lighten up.

Another text popped up from Lynx when Yanni went to the restroom. She hurried to respond.

Checking on you.

I'm good. Out with my sister. TTYL.

OK. Wanted to come over tonight.

Tomorrow is better.

He responded with a sad-face emoji. Shanna sent him emojis with three hearts and kisses.

Some would call her prudish, but she wouldn't allow Lynx to sleep over with Yanni in the house. Not that her sister would mind. Shanna didn't want Yanni using that as a precedent to do the same. Her sister had a liberal attitude toward sex and dating, and Shanna wasn't evolved enough to support an open-door policy. She would explain it to him later. He had younger siblings and should understand her decision.

I'll come early.

What about work?

I still have vacation time.

Oh yes. She had forgotten her dilemma had in-terrupted his two-week vacation plans. Since she wouldn't be working, he must have reclaimed his break.

Bring breakfast.

Lynx sent a picture of an eggplant, and Shanna busted into laughter. Of course her sister *would* choose that moment to return. Curious, Yanni tried to grab Shanna's phone but Shanna had good reflexes.

She twisted around so Yanni couldn't see.

That works too.

She added kissing lips and hit Send, imagining Lynx's reaction. She squeezed her legs tight. Tomorrow couldn't come soon enough.

Yanni told her she was going to wait on Daniel instead of going home. After asking if she had protection, warning her to be careful and to text her whereabouts, and then making sure Yanni turned on the Find My iPhone feature, Shanna drove home alone.

When she put her key in the door, she felt an odd sensation. Almost as if she was being watched. She turned around and called out, "Hello?" but there was no one there. Berating herself and calling herself all kinds of a fool, Shanna went inside and locked the door behind her.

Chapter Twenty-Seven

Lynx put the burner dial on its lowest setting and added a small amount of butter to the pan. He finished beating four eggs and poured the mixture into the pan, adding salt and pepper. The secret to beautiful scrambled eggs was low heat.

When he woke up that morning, Lynx realized that Shanna had never been to his house, and he wanted to remedy that. He had called Shanna to invite her over, offering to make her breakfast and including a not-so-subtle hint to pack an overnight bag with a bathing suit. He couldn't wait to see her in his space and planned for them to go out on his boat later.

The *Boston Whaler Dauntless* was ideal for fishing and watersports and had been a gift from his brother Axel when Lynx had made the principalship. He didn't use it much, but today would be a good day for boating. It was raining now, but the sun would be out by midafternoon.

After showering and dressing in shorts and a T-shirt, Lynx had started on breakfast.

He put on the teakettle and checked the turkey sausage he had seasoned with salt and pepper before slipping it in the oven. He sniffed, appreciating the smell of the sausage, which was getting crisp around the edges, just the way he liked.

Opening the cupboard to the left of the stove, Lynx reached for two plates, two teacups and two water glasses. Then he got two sets of utensils. Laying them on the counter, he smiled. It was nice to be setting things up for two instead of one.

Lynx yawned, emitting a sound that would do a lion proud. He hadn't slept well. His father's ultimatum had plagued his mind before he decided Shanna's well-being was more important than the superintendent position. Lynx had picked up his cell phone numerous times to call her, but he wanted the deadbeat who was causing her trouble to be caught. She wouldn't be good at playing dumb, and worse— he could see her plotting to capture the troublemaker herself. His woman, who proclaimed she didn't need rescuing. So he didn't tell her. Instead, he would keep her close.

His woman. He liked the sound of that. Knowing she was with Yanni was the sole reason he hadn't sat watch outside her house last night.

He dropped four pieces of bread in the toaster, and placed a small dish of butter on top of the toaster to warm. That would help it to spread smoothly across the bread. His doorbell rang just as he had plated their food.

Lynx wiped his hands on one of the towels hanging on the handle of the oven. Spotting the spare key, he slipped it into his pocket and rushed to answer the door.

Shanna was wearing a white T-shirt and a pair of unbuttoned jean shorts. The rain had dampened the shirt, and he could see a red bikini top underneath. He wanted to rip off her shirt and love on her until she hollered for mercy, but he knew she had to be hungry for an actual breakfast, and he didn't want her to think he only wanted her body.

She gave him a knowing smile. "Are you going to let me in?"

He stepped aside.

"I'm sorry. I was too busy gawking at you to remember my manners." He closed the door behind him and took the overnight bag out of her hand. "Make yourself at home. I'll be right back." Lynx went into his bedroom and placed her bag by the bed. He would give her a tour after they ate.

He heard a door close. Shanna had found the half bath. He should have anticipated that and showed her where it was located.

While she freshened up, he placed their plates on the table, made hot chocolate and poured orange juice. Shanna walked in and raised her brows. "This looks wonderful."

"Thanks. I hope you're hungry."

"*Ummm-hmm.* I don't think I said hello," she said, coming over to give him a kiss. It was short and sweet and left him wanting more. He gave her a quick tour of the interior of his home, ending in the kitchen. Then he held out the chair for her to take a seat before pulling his chair so close to hers, their elbows bumped. His leg brushed against hers while they ate.

Shanna ate the last piece of turkey sausage, licked her lips and gave a satisfied sigh. "That was some good food. You threw down."

"Besides this, I grill a mean salmon, and that's the extent of my cooking skills," Lynx said, chuckling. "What about you? Do you cook?"

"Had to," she said. "My mother worked late hours, and my sister and I had to eat. I've been cooking since I was twelve."

He rubbed his stomach. "Well, I'm really good at eating, so I'd say we make a great team."

She gathered their plates and placed them in the sink. He eyed her plump bottom, appreciating how it moved with the sway of her wide hips. Another hunger began to build. Lynx sauntered over and cuddled against her. She leaned into him, resting her head against his chest. He felt a sense of completeness he hadn't known he lacked. From where they stood, they could see the rain slithering down the sliding door. For several moments, they stayed wrapped in each other's arms, watching the downpour.

"When is your sister leaving for campus?" he asked, kissing her ear.

"She's already on her way. We said our goodbyes this morning," Shanna said. "It was a good thing she was already packed for school, because she didn't come home last night."

He stilled. That meant she had been on her own, and that lunatic could've gotten inside her house and done her harm. He must have tightened his hold, because Shanna tapped his arm. "You're cutting off my air."

"I'm sorry," he said, fighting the urge to express his frustration. He needed to tell her what was going on. But it would freak her out. While his mind churned, she swiveled to face him. She wore no makeup, and her hair was in a messy bun, but to Lynx, she was beautiful. He didn't think he would tire of looking at her.

"So where's that eggplant you said you had to show me? I'm still hungry." She winked at him.

Those words shifted his mind, stirring the embers of his ever-present need for her. "I'll show you in a minute." He leaned over to give her a tender kiss, moving slow, teasing her. The patter of the rain mingled with the sounds of their breathing.

Hoisting her in his arms, he placed her on the countertop, positioning her so her head wouldn't hit the lights. He appreciated her chest heaving with each breath she took. He lifted her shirt off, and his breath caught. He didn't know how that scrap of red was holding up those double Ds. The color popped against her skin.

"Can I ban you from wearing bikinis in public?" he asked.

She giggled. "You're so silly. This is rated PG compared to what other girls are wearing, and I'm fully covered."

"It's not what you're wearing—it's who's wearing it." Lynx tossed the bikini top across the floor, loving on her, until she was hot for him.

He reached for her shorts next. Shanna jumped off the counter so he could take them off. "Don't you want to go into the bedroom?" she asked, huffing.

"No. I plan to have my meal right here," he said before lowering her back onto the countertop, removing the rest of her clothes and proceeded to feast. Shanna arched her back and screamed. Her scent was an aphrodisiac. His body yearned for completion, but he waited for her to reach the ultimate satisfaction.

After, Lynx lifted her languid body and took her into his bedroom. He took a moment to observe her flushed cheeks, her matted hair against her face, before he kissed her long and hard. "You're exquisite," he said.

"Oh goodness, Lynx. That was… That was…" She exhaled. "I don't even have the words."

While he undressed, she got out of bed. A few seconds later, he heard the ice machine. She returned with a glass of water. She took a few sips before offering him the glass. He declined, moving to lay on the bed.

Shanna took an ice cube into her mouth and scooted close to him. He jumped when her cold hand touched his chest. She bit back a smile, and he realized she had done that on purpose. With the ice cube in her mouth, she trailed kisses down his chest, moving lower.

What she did next made his toes curl. Her lips drove him to the point of madness. The ice melted, and like a siren, she crawled up his chest, never breaking eye contact. Lynx flipped her to her back and took over. With powerful strokes, he urged her, "Come with me, baby. Come."

She bit her lower lip, curved her body and rode with him until they both found sweet release. He moved off her and tucked her into his chest.

"That was amazing," she said.

"Yes, it was." He snuggled her close before sitting up to face her.

Her eyelids looked heavy, and she gave him a sleepy smile. He shook her lightly. "Hey, I have to tell you something before you go to sleep."

She raised herself on her arms, and he helped her to sit up. "What is it? Is something wrong?"

"No, nothing's wrong," he said, cupping her face. "Everything is right." His mind told him not to say a word, that it was too fast, but his heart bid him to speak. "I need to tell you something." He cleared his throat. Myriad thoughts raced through his mind before common sense prevailed. "I know this is going to seemed rush, and it's only been a few days, but I want us to be exclusive. I want to have a relationship with you. I'm hoping you want the same, because this time, I won't muck this up."

She nodded. "I want that too."

He hugged her close. That wasn't what he wanted to say. He wanted to tell her he had fallen in love with her, but he sensed Shanna needed time—time to believe him because she knew he'd just broken up with his girlfriend. Telling her he loved her might be seen as a red flag. His heart needed to wait for hers to catch up.

In the meantime, he didn't have to utter the words to show her how he felt. His actions could do all the talking. Besides, declaring his love right after love-making might not have the same effect. He should tell her when they were both clearheaded and not reeling under the haze of fulfillment.

Yes, he told himself. That was the right thing to do.

Chapter Twenty-Eight

Shanna studied Lynx from under her lashes, sipping on her bottled water. His chiseled body and six-pack abs glistened as he maneuvered the boat across the water. The sun had come out, and they were headed toward a cool spot he had to show her.

They had taken a quick shower in Lynx's oversize bathroom, dressed in their same clothes from earlier and cleaned up the kitchen. She loved how they worked in sync. Before they left, they had made sure to apply a generous amount of sunscreen. He had the boat stored in his garage since it was hurricane season. Watching his muscles bulge while he rubbed the sunscreen into his back and arms had been something to see.

Right now, the waters were warm and calm, so it

was a smooth ride. Water sprayed, dampening her curls. She made sure to put on her life jacket and seat belt. He dipped into an inlet and dropped anchor.

She looked at the grass, standing tall like stalks of corn, and shook her head. "I don't see anything."

Lynx walked over to her and twisted her body until she faced the other direction. "Some of the best things in life are right behind us. We just have to turn around to see."

Her breath caught, and she covered her mouth with a hand. The horizon had shades of blue, and bright clouds blended with orange, reds and slivers of gray. A couple of birds added to the picture that would be forever frozen in her mind. The sun was at half-mast, and there was a peace she couldn't explain that surrounded her. She tilted her head back, admiring the glory of the painter with the world's largest paintbrush. "Wow. That's majestic."

He nodded. "The first time I saw this, I almost spoke in tongues."

She chuckled. "Wait. What do you know about that?"

"I went to a black church," he said, doing a jig. "I know all about the praise break." Shanna joined him with a quick two-step, and they shared a laugh. Pointing to the sky, Lynx asked, "Do you see the rainbow?"

Shanna shook her head.

He said, "Look behind the clouds. It's faint, but it's there."

She squinted. There was a shard of deep purple

and light yellows with a small halo. "I see it. I see the rainbow."

"I know this is going to sound corny, but I come here in moments when I don't know what to do or when I'm facing my greatest disappointments. I come here because I always end up seeing something—*feeling* something—that gives me hope." He cradled her against him.

She leaned into him. "I feel a peace when I'm with you that I can't quantify or express."

He squeezed her shoulders. "I know what you mean. I'm not a poetic man, but you make me feel things and say things I wouldn't normally feel or say."

"Who would have known?" she said. "If it weren't for this scandal, I wouldn't be here with you right now."

"See what I mean?" he said. "Something about this place brings out the positive vibes and makes you see things from another perspective." Shanna believed it had something to do with getting away from the busy that was the world and taking a moment to find solitude. His voice lowered, and he turned her so they could see eye to eye. "I need you to know I've never brought another woman here—make that another *person*. This is my place—my escape—but I felt compelled to share it with you." He dug into his shorts to pull out a key, which glinted in the sun. "This is the key to my house. I want you to have it. You're welcome into my place anytime. You don't even have to call first. Having you with me today made me understand when other people talk about making a house a home. You're my home, Shanna."

Her eyes welled. She took the key and placed it inside the pocket of her tiny shorts. "Thank you for opening up to me. I haven't been in too many relationships because I've always been about school or work or taking care of my mom and sister. With you, I don't have to do anything. I just have to be. Do you know how much I treasure that?"

He kissed her long and slow, and they swayed with the movement of the boat. Shanna wished the moment would never end.

"Remember when you asked me about my favorite flower?" she asked.

"Yeah. You said you didn't have one."

She pointed to a bed of lotus flowers. "I think I now have a favorite."

"Good choice. It blooms even when it's in muddy waters."

Shanna retrieved her cell phone. "I don't have any reception."

"Yeah, the connection isn't good out here."

Shanna captured pictures of the horizon, the flowers, and of her and Lynx, especially when he dropped his shorts and revealed skimpy black trunks he declared were for her eyes only.

And her eyes did enjoy exploring his firm butt, his noticeable bulge and those strong, firm thighs. He executed a perfect dive and went into the water. She placed the phone on the seat before joining him to frolic. The sun had made the water about seventy-five degrees. They played Marco Polo like they were children, except their prize involved kisses and secret touches under the water.

Since they hadn't packed anything in the cooler but water, they left a couple hours later. Swimming has a way of making you hungry. They left the idyllic hideaway and returned to Lynx's house.

As soon as they did, both their cell phones went off with a frenzy. She had missed calls and text messages.

"It's my father," he said. "He's called me at least three times."

"And my sister is trying to reach me." She left Lynx in the living area and scampered into the bedroom to give her sister a call. The phone barely rang once before Yanni picked up.

"Where have you been?" Yanni said, sounding like she was hyperventilating.

"I was out with Lynx on his boat. There's no service out where we were. We just got back, and my phone went crazy with alerts." Shanna's legs weakened, and she sank to the edge of the bed. "What's the matter? What's going on?" If something had happened to Yanni while she was out, Shanna would never forgive herself.

"Have you watched the news?" Yanni asked, frantic. "Turn on the television and turn to LCN. Oh my goodness. They've been playing the breaking news on repeat. I'm glad you're okay. When I didn't get you, I thought... I didn't know what to think." Yanni drew in small, deep breaths.

Shanna searched for the remote and turned on the television. She flipped to the Love Creek News and turned up the volume.

"Are you seeing it?" Yanni asked.

"Not yet. Can you just tell me?" she asked, losing patience. Yanni tended to be dramatic, so she hoped her sister hadn't alarmed her for something minor, even as she prayed it was minor.

"The police just arrested your former assistant principal Todd Smith for stalking and for threatening your life. They were searching for you because they thought he had you hostage when no one could reach you and you weren't at your house."

Her mouth hung open. "Say what? Todd? My assistant principal?" Her heart thumped as her mind sought to process all that her sister had said. "What has he done?"

Just then, she saw her face across the screen. "Wait. I see it." She yelled out to Lynx to come into the bedroom and increased the volume even more. He rushed inside to hear the anchor begin. He still had his cell pressed to his ear, so she figured his father had given him the same news.

"The police have taken the former assistant principal of River's Edge, Todd Smith, into custody. He has been charged with conspiracy and possibly abduction if Ms. Shanna Jacobs cannot be found."

Shanna gasped when her picture graced the screen once more. Seeing her face on display jarred her senses.

"If you remember, Shanna Jacobs, principal of

River's Edge, had been recently placed on administrative leave pending an investigation into suspicions that she spearheaded one of the biggest cheating scandals in the history of the small town." The camera zoomed in on the reporter. "As a result of that investigation, Todd Smith was terminated along with a few others."

Shanna's eyes went wide as she grappled with disbelief. She couldn't believe Todd wanted to harm her.

"Police state that Todd Smith, diagnosed with an undisclosed mental condition, snapped. When they searched his home, police found dozens of handwritten notes in which Mr. Smith blames Principal Jacobs for his downfall, saying she pushed them to get higher scores."

Shanna's mouth dropped. Instead of accepting responsibility, Todd was blaming her for what he'd done. *Wow.*

"We will keep you informed as more details emerge. Stay tuned." The anchor moved on to a story about a bear-spotting.

Her heart thumped, her hands felt sweaty and her legs were like eels. She had to keep a tight grip on the cell phone. "I have to call the police and let them know I am okay." Even saying the words made her quiver. She had never had any dealings with law enforcement—and didn't want to, either. But she had to let them know she was safe.

"Yes, I'll call you later. I can breathe now that I know you're alive." Yanni sobbed. "I was so worried. I don't know what I would have done without you. I love you, big sis."

She took several minutes to get Yanni calm, giving her repeated assurances that she was indeed fine. It was only when Shanna reminded Yanni again she needed to contact law enforcement that Yanni allowed her to end the call.

"I'll call them for you," Lynx said.

Shanna nodded, her mind filled with the revelation that Todd Smith, a man she had mentored and hired, had wanted her dead. The realization left her chilled. She rubbed her arms. Lynx reentered and held out his hands. "I convinced them to wait until tomorrow before coming to see you."

Grateful, she raced into his arms, inhaling his scent, which mingled with that of the water. She felt secure, steady, and drew from his strength when he tightened his hold.

He patted her on the back. "I'm so glad this is finally over. You'll be able to resume your duties this fall without missing a beat." Then he gave her a tender kiss.

Something about his words gave her pause, but Shanna was too busy enjoying the feel of his lips against hers, and the newness of their relationship, to give the matter much consideration.

Her cell phone went off, and she broke the kiss. "I'd better get that. It could be the nursing home."

It was Laurie.

"Okay. I'm going to get into the shower," he said. She nodded and mouthed, "I'll miss you." Even though he was only going a few feet away, she missed his presence already. She would love to watch him lather himself and run his hands over his body. Add that attraction to her emotions, and Shanna diagnosed herself with a bad case of lub. *Lub* was a term she and Laurie had concocted for when feelings for a man felt like they were in between lust and love.

Her best friend squealed once she answered the phone. "Oh, thank my lucky stars you picked up the phone. I thought Craig and I would have to come hunting for you."

Shanna frowned. "Craig? I thought you two were over."

"Yeah." Laurie giggled. "We patched things up."

"Are you sure that's the right thing to do?"

"Let's keep this about you. Are you okay?"

Because she knew Laurie's concern came from a place of genuineness, Shanna dropped the discussion of Laurie and Craig's reunion. But that wouldn't be the end of it. Craig Marshall was not the man he portrayed himself to be. However, that wasn't a conversation to have over the phone.

"I'm okay. I had no idea this was all going on. I was out with Lynx on his boat, and we had a wonderful day. I'm actually with him still."

"Oh… You'll have to fill me in on that."

Shanna smiled at the inflection in Laurie's tone. She knew her friend would want to know every single detail. "Let's catch up tomorrow," she said, already looking forward to their conversation. "We can make a day of it. I have to get a mani-pedi."

"Okay. It's a date. Smooches."

After blowing Laurie kisses, she ended the call. Shanna moseyed toward the bathroom. She had started to undress, anticipating showering with Lynx, when she froze. Lynx's words from a few minutes ago replayed in her mind: *I'm so glad this is finally over.* Spotting his phone on the floor, she picked it up, put it in her pocket and made her way into the bathroom.

He was whistling off-key to a tune she didn't recognize but stopped and gave her a wide smile. "Coming in?" he asked, wiping the fog off the shower to waggle his eyebrows at her.

She was tempted to help him wash that delectable body, but she had to address the question niggling her mind. "What did you mean when you said you were glad this was finally over?"

"Hmm?" he asked, using a loofah to scrub his back. The scent of his Axe Phoenix body wash filled the room.

She walked closer to the shower. "Your words made it seem like you already knew something. Like this was more than just about the scandal. Did you?"

Chapter Twenty-Nine

Lynx slowly turned the handle to the off position, then stepped out of the shower and onto the large mat. He reached for one of the oversize towels that hung on his shower door and wrapped it around his waist. His eyes never left those of the woman standing on the other side of the room, tapping her foot and awaiting his response. He walked across the tiles, debating the best approach to answer the question.

He had no intention of lying, but he could kick himself for his choice of words. But a relationship wouldn't survive if it began on a poor foundation.

"I did know something," he said. "My father told me yesterday."

Her brows rose to her forehead. "Why didn't you tell me?"

"He asked me not to because, according to him, the cops had it handled. He didn't want you freaking out."

"While the cops used me as bait?" she asked, heat building in her eyes. "Would they have done this if I were a different shade?"

He shifted, hating the connotation behind her words. "I don't think they saw it that way. Race had nothing to do with this. They wanted to catch that psycho before he harmed you," he said, placing his hands on both her shoulders. He could feel her shaking under his grip. "It's over now. That's the main thing."

He started to get goose bumps, so he left the bathroom and walked into his bedroom. Shanna followed him.

"That's not the main thing. I should have known if someone was after me. And forgive me if I don't think this is about race. When you're brown like me, race is never *not* an issue."

He whipped off the towel and dried off, then put on a pair of shorts. "I agree that might be the case ninety percent of the time, but there are rare times like this one where I don't believe it was about the color of your skin. I think it falls in that ten percent. My father is black, and I think he would agree."

She snorted and rolled her eyes. "I'm not going to argue with you about something you have no idea about." She cocked her head. "Is that why you heeded your father's advice against warning me?"

This was the inquiry he'd been dreading. He

wiped his face and cleared his throat. "My father threatened me with taking away the superintendent position if I told you."

Her mouth hung open. Then, after she'd recovered: "Wow. I see where I stand with you when it counts."

The pain in her voice hit his heart with the accuracy of a sharpshooter. Lynx hated the tears that formed in her eyes. Worse, he hated knowing he'd helped put them there. When the tears rolled down her cheeks, it felt like his own heart was bleeding.

He rushed over to her. "It wasn't like that. Please don't think that, honey. I wasn't worried about you getting hurt because I had every intention of being with you twenty-four-seven. Nothing would have happened to you under my watch."

"You can't guarantee that," she said. Her lips quivered. "Now I feel like I can't trust you."

No. He couldn't lose her the same day they'd made an exclusive commitment. His heart rebelled, pleading with him to fix this. Hearing things from her point of view had showed him he had chosen the wrong option.

"I'm sorry," he said, reaching out to hold her in his arms. He kissed her forehead when she didn't pull away. "Baby, I know I didn't show it, but you mean more to me than that job."

She stiffened. Placing her hands on his chest, she said, "I don't believe you. When it came down to it, your job was your priority. A part of me gets that. I'm just as ambitious as you are, but not at the cost of someone else's life. That was the difference you didn't consider."

With a shake of her head, Shanna turned away from him. "I'm going home. I need space to think."

"Baby, don't go. Please." He poured all the emotion he could into those few words. "We're a couple now. We need to hash this out, use it as a learning experience for our relationship moving forward."

Shanna appeared to consider his words. He watched the myriad expressions on her face and prayed his words had reached her. He could see she was torn, and so he pleaded, "Yell at me. Be mad with me, but don't leave. Stay."

Her shoulders curved, and she took a step.

Just as she did, his cell phone went off.

Shanna pulled it out of her shorts and handed it to him. Irene had called him using FaceTime. He wanted to press the decline button, prepared to have the call go to voice mail. He had no time to deal with Irene and her theatrics. They were over. Nothing more needed to be said between them.

"Go ahead and answer it," she dared.

If he didn't, Shanna would believe he had something to hide. So Lynx answered and placed the call on speaker. Irene's voice blasted through the room.

"Care to tell me why a picture of you and some *chic-ho* are all over the internet?" she hurled out.

Shanna gasped. She opened her mouth, but Lynx held up a hand to keep her from interfering. Irene was his mess to handle.

"Don't you dare come out your face and call her

that name," Lynx said, his voice filled with steel. "We're over. Don't call me anymore."

"Really? This is how you humiliate me?" Irene raged, baring her teeth. She pointed her index finger close to the screen, bringing her face closer so that she appeared distorted.

Sure enough, Irene had made this about her.

"I'm getting off the phone now. Have a nice life."

He was just about to end the call when Irene yelled, "We'll see what your girl thinks when she sees I was in your bed last week. It's all over Twitter."

Lynx pressed End as the rocks piled into his stomach. He looked at Shanna and said, "I can explain."

Shanna shook her head. "Your ex-girlfriend was here? In your bed? Days after we made love? What kind of game are you playing? I don't do cat and mouse, so you can play this game by yourself."

"Yes, she was here. But give me a chance to—"

Her eyes became like glass stones and her face a mask. Her calm scared him. "Don't say another word to me." She shook her head. "You almost had me going, there, with your sad eyes, but that call came right on time. I don't ever want to see you again."

That would be impossible since they worked for the same district, but Lynx knew better than to say that.

"I won't stop you if you want to go. But at least hear me out before you go through that door, because I'm not the man she's making me out to be."

Shanna shook her head. "I think you've said and done enough to last me a lifetime. It doesn't matter if you're not the man she's making you out to be. I could care less. What matters is the man I see before me doesn't have a problem telling me half-truths or keeping things from me. And that's not a man I care to know."

Calm as the eye of a hurricane, she gathered her belongings and departed his house. She didn't holler or scream, but her silence ripped at him, tearing at his heart. Her exit sucked all the zest and oxygen out of his house. He felt stifled, wandering through the rooms, seeing her everywhere. He would have driven to his parents' house, but he'd spotted the media skulking around, waiting. Caged, Lynx took refuge in his workroom. He puttered around his space and searched auction sites for his grandfather's watch, but he couldn't concentrate.

Without her there, his place felt sterile.

Silent.

The silence got to him when it never had before. He had six brothers he could call, but he decided on Hawk, who was in Miami, hitting up the clubs with some of his teammates. Lynx declined the invite to join them, but they made plans to meet up the next day.

Next, he called his mother.

She sided with Shanna on everything before advising him to give her time or let her go. He lost his breath when she said that.

"I love her," Lynx confessed, pouring out the truth from his heart. "I've always known. Deep down.

From a teen, she was the one. I was just too stubborn to admit it."

"Did you tell her?"

"No. I asked her if we could be exclusive. I figured I would wait until she was ready before telling her."

"There you go again, son—talking for her. Thinking for her. She doesn't need you to do any of that. Just love her."

He dragged his hands through his hair and paced inside his kitchen. "I made a mess of this."

"Yes, you did. So do what you do best, son. Fix it." With that, Tanya got off the phone.

Lynx's mind churned on it for most of the night before an idea formed. He had a plan. For the first time in hours, he smiled.

Chapter Thirty

Two empty tubs of ice cream—one butter pecan and the other, cookie dough—lay on the coffee table, joined by chocolate syrup, maraschino cherries, crushed walnuts and whipped cream.

Shanna and Laurie were both stretched out on their backs on Shanna's couch in her small living area. Since Cooper was still in California, Laurie had come prepared to spend the night. Shanna held a bag of Crunchy Cheetos and Laurie, a bag of Cool Ranch Doritos. *10 Things I Hate About You*, starring Julia Stiles and Heath Ledger, played for a second time on the forty-eight-inch television. Neither woman was watching. Both had their eyes glued to their phones, reading Lynx's ex-girlfriend Irene's Twitter rants.

The younger woman—who Laurie had dubbed

the Prawn—had posted a suggestive photo of her in Lynx's bed, calling him a cheat and Shanna a whore. Shanna and Laurie had investigated the photo numerous times through the evening. As soon as Shanna left Lynx, she had called Laurie, who arrived minutes after her, and their gorge-fest had begun. It was now well past midnight, and after another crying session, they had returned to Twitter to find more posts. Each one seemed crazier than the next.

"You might need to get the police involved," Laurie said, shaking her head.

"She's not worth it," Shanna said, looking her friend's way. "I have to believe this will all blow over and I can return to my normal life."

Laurie's head snapped up. "Are you sure you want normal?"

"Very sure. After the day I've had, give me dull, droll, uneventful. That's what I crave right now."

"And what about Lynx?" Laurie asked. She swung her legs to the floor and brushed the Doritos crumbs off her leggings.

"I told you, I'm done with him."

"Just like that, huh?" Laurie snapped her fingers.

"Yep. Just like that." Shanna bent over to put the Cheetos on the coffee table. The tips of her fingers were orange with bits of fake cheese stuck to them. When she was a kid, she would have sucked the orange goop off each finger. She grabbed the last tissue from the box and wiped her hands; then she straightened and tucked her feet under her.

Shanna felt Laurie's eyes on her. "What?" she asked.

"I think you're making a big mistake," Laurie said. "In fact, I know you are."

"He lied to me," she said, pointing to her chest. "You expect me to let that go?"

"Naw, girl. This isn't about that, and you know it." Laurie scooted close to her, hitting Shanna with her Doritos breath. "This is about you not trusting any man. You were looking for a reason to let Lynx go. The minute he got too close, you were ready for him to go."

Shanna strove to control her temper. "That's not true. This isn't about my father." Though, in the back of her mind, she wondered if Laurie was right. Maybe her father was at the root of her trust issues. "I agreed to a commitment—and the same day, I learned Lynx was holding things back from me. And he slept with Irene right after he was with me. What does that say about his character?"

Laurie shook her head. "I don't believe you, of all people, have condemned him without asking questions. All those years you held a grudge against him because he misjudged you. Now look at you. You're doing the same thing."

"It's not the same thing." Her chest heaved. She glared at Laurie. "I don't like you sometimes."

"No, but you love me. I wouldn't be a friend if I didn't tell you the truth, and the truth is that that woman is spiteful. Her head ain't wrapped too tight.

Lynx isn't anywhere in that picture. For all we know, Irene could be making the whole thing up."

"It doesn't matter. We're done. I'm not risking my heart over someone who might not deserve it." She folded her arms around herself.

"Are you sure?" Laurie asked. "Love isn't common. It's as rare as a Stresemann's bristlefront."

"What's that?" Shanna asked, rolling her eyes. She bet it was some random fact Cooper had taught her. Her godson had a mild case of Asperger's and loved to share interesting facts.

"It's a rare bird," Laurie explained, wiping at her brow. "Cooper told me about it."

"So you're saying love is a rare bird."

"Yes. So when you find it, you should grab on to it."

Shanna raised a brow. "Put it in a cage?"

Laurie cracked up. Shanna joined her. "Whatever. You get the point." Then she grew serious. "You're beautiful and talented, and I don't want you to end up alone." She held up a hand before Shanna could respond. "And before you say anything, let me clarify. There's nothing wrong if you're single by choice, but if that's not your choice, then compromise and communication is a must for any relationship to work."

"It didn't work for my mother," Shanna said as the tears banked up behind her lids. "She compromised. She worked hard. She communicated. She did everything right, and my dad still left."

Laurie moved to hug her, and Shanna's restraint broke.

"It doesn't mean Lynx will do the same," her friend said.

"I'm scared," she said, crying into Laurie's shoulder. "I don't think I can do this."

"You can." Laurie pulled away and placed a finger to lift Shanna's chin. "You deserve to be loved just like anyone else. You're worth loving. That's why I love you so much."

The thought of Lynx with anyone else made her heart burn. She chewed on her bottom lip. "Thanks for loving me. I love you, too, and I really appreciate the great advice."

"You're welcome, love. I'm pretty good at giving it. Maybe one day, I'll listen to myself."

Shanna pondered on Laurie's words through most of the night. Her friend left early the next morning, after urging Shanna to reach out to Lynx—give him a second chance. Shanna watched Laurie's Prius back out of the driveway, knowing she wouldn't.

Her conversation with Laurie had made Shanna see that she had more baggage than she'd realized. The superintendent had called that very morning to set up a meeting two weeks away. She presumed it was to discuss her return to her admin duties. Shanna had already decided she would remain on leave. She had been there for her sister, for her friend and for her mother. It was time for Shanna to be there for herself.

Then, and only then, could she think about Lynx. *He might move on*, her heart fretted.

She lifted her chin. Love was a risk. She loved herself enough to take that risk.

Chapter Thirty-One

"You look like crap turned over," Hawk said, standing at his door the next morning. He wore a tan fishing hat, huge sunglasses, a white T-shirt, red shorts and matching red sneakers. Hawk had a sneaker fetish. He had several pairs of the same sneakers and often purchased them in different colors.

"That's a bad analogy," Lynx said, stepping aside to let his big brother inside. He was also dressed in a hat, plain white tee, jeans and an old pair of sneakers. Hawk dropped an army bag to the floor.

"That's how bad you look." Hawk pulled him into his huge chest for a hug, using one arm like he had when they were kids; then he wiped his sneakers on the mat.

Lynx scratched at his day-old beard and yawned.

"If you had the night I had, you would look the same."

"Naw, bro. That's never going to happen." Hawk shook his head. "You have scared me off love. Look at you." Lynx had filled Hawk in on everything while his brother drove up from Miami. He appreciated Hawk taking the time to come see him.

"Bro, I have to agree. I can't even work on my watches, man. I ended up calling the cops on Irene like you suggested."

His brother gave him a look filled with sympathy. "That was a good move. She can't get away with dragging you through the mud like that. That's cyberbullying or harassment."

They made their way to the kitchen. Hawk zoned in on the table. "I drove three hours and through Alligator Alley to come see you, so I'm glad you decided to feed me."

"I got you." Lynx pointed to the table, where he had several bagels, cream cheese, orange juice and boiled eggs.

"All right. That's what I'm talking about." Hawk went to the sink and poured a small amount of dishwashing liquid in his hands before washing them; then he helped himself to a whole wheat bagel and two boiled eggs. Hawk placed his bagel in the toaster. He drummed his fingers on the granite countertop while he waited.

Lynx placed two eggs on his plate and chose a cinnamon-raisin bagel. After spreading a generous amount of cream cheese on it, he took a bite.

"Tell me about this plan of yours," Hawk said once his bagel was ready and he had joined Lynx at the kitchen table.

"We're going to restore her mother's fountain. It's an eyesore in front of her yard, but since her mother adored it, she wants to keep it. It's cracked and in need of repair." Lynx jutted his chin toward Hawk. "That's where you come in. You're the best at cementing and working with sculptures."

When they were young, Hawk used to do cement work at construction sites before he got into sculpting. He hand-sculpted all sorts of pieces, and each of the brothers had something of Hawk's made especially with them in mind. Of course, Lynx had a sculpture of the animal whose name he bore, which he kept in his workroom. It was one of the last pieces Hawk had made.

"I'm also cheap labor," Hawk said, shaking his head. "I haven't made anything like that in a while. Not since—" He stopped, refusing to utter his ex's name.

"I know I'm asking a lot, but I really need your help."

"I really want to help, but I don't know if I can do this," Hawk said.

Lynx leaned forward and pressed his case. "Sculpting is your second love—next to football. It's time to rekindle that love affair, rediscover if you've still got it."

Hawk nodded. A nod was as good as his word.

"Thanks, man." Lynx swallowed to keep from

getting too emotional. "I don't know what else to do to show her how I feel."

He tensed, waiting for Hawk to rag on him, but his brother merely smiled.

"We're going to need to get supplies, and I'll have to see the piece. Prepare yourself, and don't get your hopes up. It might not be fit for repair, and the cement will have to cure for at least a week before I can work on the fountain."

"I actually want you to talk me through how to do it. I want to fix it with my own two hands. I'll see if I can get another week off from work," Lynx said. "It shouldn't be a problem. I usually lose vacation days, so HR will be happy to see me use them."

"We'll do it together," Hawk said. "Will she let us on her property? I love you, but I don't want to go to jail for trespassing. And come to think of it, didn't she say she didn't want to see you again?"

"Yes, she did, but don't worry. I've got it handled." Lynx hadn't thought of the trespassing factor, but he was sure his father would help him out—lure Shanna away for a day. She couldn't report him for trespassing if she didn't see him. He wiped his brow. Reality was different from fairy tales. The hero never had to worry about ending up with charges for doing a good deed in the name of true love.

Lynx added, "While we're working on the fountain, I have a crew coming to landscape her entire yard. This job would take more than a day, so I hired extra manpower to get it done. I'll change the appointment to next week."

It had cost him a few thousand dollars to get this task completed in a single day. He was using the funds he had earmarked to purchase his grandfather's watch, but Shanna was worth that and more.

"Wow. Talk about go big or go home," Hawk said. "I'm impressed. Do you need me to spot you some cash?"

"More like putting my money where my mouth—or in this case, my heart—is. But, no, thanks. I've got to do this myself."

Hawk scrunched his nose. "I can't help but mention that renovating her yard is a cheaper option than getting her an engagement ring."

Lynx saw his brother's teasing eyes and chuckled. "You might take that back once you've seen her fortress, because that's what it is. Trust me when I say Shanna will love this."

He hoped.

She had already accused him of presuming to think and talk for her. His stomach muscles tensed. But from how she talked about her mother and that fountain, there was no way she would misinterpret his intentions.

With his brother around, Lynx didn't have time to mope or feel sorry for himself. But it gave him a not-always-willing participant to listen as he cited Shanna's desirable qualities. Poor Hawk. It got so bad, he made Lynx promise not to bring her up for even one day. But apparently talking about *not* talking about her was still talking about her. Somehow, Shanna's name made it in every conversation.

At Lowe's.

At the supermarket.

During a movie.

On the boat.

Playing basketball.

Everywhere and everything circled back to Shanna. By the end of the week, Hawk was rooting for Lynx, if only to get him to shut up about Shanna Jacobs.

Fortunately, he had gotten other things done. Lynx had served Irene with a cease-and-desist order with a stipulation that if she didn't remove her postings, she would be charged with harassment. After calling him a first-class jerk, Irene had pulled that picture off social media and deleted her tweets. Not that it made a difference, because the photograph was already out there. He had also fixed the watch he had purchased in North Carolina and presented it to Hawk as an early birthday gift.

But the most wonderful thing was seeing Hawk sculpt again. His brother had made a squirrel and a few garden stones to add to Lynx's yard.

Before he knew it, it was Tuesday and time to execute his plan. Hawk wished him luck, but Lynx had only one wish, and that was for Shanna to accept the gift of his heart.

Chapter Thirty-Two

Shanna dressed with care Tuesday morning for her meeting with Lynx's mom. Tanya had called to invite Shanna to her home. Shanna had been surprised at the other woman's call, but she couldn't think of a reason to decline. Besides, she had known Tanya Harrington since she was a child. She had asked what the meeting was about, but Tanya had only said to dress casually. So Shanna had chosen a pair of black jeans, a white blouse and a black short-sleeved blazer.

Over the past week, Shanna had made some impactful decisions. She had put in to resume her doctoral program. She knew that things would get hectic once she began working on the interior of her house, but she was sure she would be able to handle the workload. Shanna had stripped the old wallpaper and painted her bedroom.

Next, Shanna had consulted with men at Lowe's to redo the bathrooms. Imagine her surprise when she learned most of what she needed done could be finished in a matter of days and not weeks. She had withdrawn the money from her savings to cover the costs now that she knew she would have her job. After two busy days, both bathrooms had been modernized. The master bath now boasted a larger shower with a smaller basin, and the other bathroom had a new tub, tiles and shower door. Yanni had been ecstatic with the changes when Shanna FaceTimed her to show her the new renovations.

That morning, Shanna had spent at least twenty minutes under the heated spray in the shower, enjoying the pulsing on her back. Her next task was to tackle the backyard and that eyesore of a fountain in the front of the house.

Shanna grabbed an apple, put on her sneakers and went outside into the muggy air. She avoided looking at the fountain and got into her vehicle. She didn't plan to be gone long because she had an important shipment coming and needed to be present to sign. She had already missed the UPS man, and he had left a note stating he would be back between 7:00 and 8:00 p.m. She put the address to Lynx's parents' home in Google Maps and followed the directions.

On the way there, she thought about Lynx.

Anytime she had a free moment, he filled her mind. During the day, she was active, in constant motion; but at night, when all was still, Shanna played back their time together. She reread their text messages and scanned their pictures before crying herself to sleep.

Her red, puffy eyes bore testament of those sleepless nights. Her body tortured her, screaming for her to call him to quench the desire crawling through her, heating her blood. She ached to hear his laugh and feel his lips touch her skin.

Yet she resisted.

After the first couple of days when he had called and texted, he hadn't been in touch. To Shanna, this meant he had accepted her choice and moved on. She tossed and turned in bed, wondering if he had given up that easy because his feelings hadn't been real. Maybe he now felt a great relief that she had ended things.

Maybe he was back with Irene.

Or another woman.

Lynx had probably forgotten their time together and was making memories with someone else while she was going crazy thinking about him all the time.

She had taken a risk and had lost the man. Knowing it *could* happen wasn't the same as *having* it happen.

She was so caught up in her thoughts, she almost didn't see the light change from yellow to red. Pressing on the brakes, Shanna came to a stop with her front end beyond the crosswalk. She heaved a sigh, relieved no one had been crossing the street. Once the light switched to green, she remained alert of her surroundings until she pulled up in the superintendent's driveway.

She looked at her watch. Hopefully, she would be out of there in under two hours. Patrick came out the door to greet her.

"Shanna, I'm so glad you could make it," he said and ushered inside his house. She nodded but wondered what the superintendent was doing at home. She wasn't about to ask him, though. She followed him and greeted Tanya. Patrick excused himself to make a phone call.

Tanya then took her on a tour of her home. It took over an hour because she had a story for every room they visited. *Every* room. For some reason, she also felt the need to point out all of Lynx's pictures, giving her all the details on the events surrounding that particular photograph.

If this were a social call, she would be enthralled. If she and Lynx were dating, she would be enamored. As it was, seeing so many pictures of Lynx made it difficult to keep a smile on her face. When Tanya showed Shanna photo of Lynx with his medal, the other woman beamed with pride.

Shanna tried to redirect Tanya to find out the purpose for the visit.

Then Tanya insisted on making Shanna breakfast.

"What do you want to eat?" Tanya asked.

Shanna couldn't resist the older woman's charm. "Anything simple," she said.

"Nonsense," Tanya said, waving her arm. "We

can't have that. Your face looks gaunt, and you need some meat on your bones."

She scrunched her nose at Tanya's blunt words. No one had ever implied she was skinny. She might have lost a pound or two, but she had more than enough weight to spare. But she wasn't going to argue.

So within seconds, she had shed her blazer, donned an apron and was hands-deep into making dough with Tanya's guidance. Tanya had set the oven to preheat during this process. While she worked, she chatted it up with Lynx's mother—meaning Tanya asked questions and Shanna provided answers.

Lynx's mother and her behaving like good friends... Surreal.

The grandfather clock gonged.

Tanya chopped up spinach and some other greens before retrieving eggs, milk and cream. Once the dough had been placed in the refrigerator to set, Shanna grated two chunks of cheddar cheese. Tanya cracked a dozen eggs and whipped them using a whisk.

Shanna found she enjoyed hanging with the older woman. Tanya was a gifted conversationalist. Several times, Shanna had to step away to laugh at something Tanya had said to keep any body fluids out of the meal.

Tanya retrieved the dough and began to prepare two crusts for quiche. She had told Shanna she often made enough food in case one of her sons stopped by. "Patrick tells me you're going to be reinstated

as principal. He's planning to make the announcement tomorrow."

"Maybe that's what he invited me here to discuss," Shanna said, using the crook of her elbow to
wipe her face.

Tanya shrugged. For once, the other woman didn't
have a comeback. Finished with the crust, Tanya
began putting the quiche together for baking.

Patrick walked inside the kitchen and rubbed his
tummy. "I can't wait to eat." He smiled at Shanna.
"I see Tanya recruited you to help. My phone call
took longer than I thought. I wasn't sure if you'd
still be here."

"I'm sorry..." She hoped she wasn't intruding on
their private time. Although Tanya had invited her...

He held up a hand. "No need to apologize. I was
just making an observation. I'm glad you're helping
so I don't have to."

"*Hmmm*... Let's see how you feel when it's time
to eat," Tanya teased.

Shanna chuckled and relaxed her shoulders.
"Well, I'm glad you're here because I have to leave
soon. I have some errands I have to run."

He looked at his watch and shook his head.

Shanna frowned at his actions.

Tanya placed a hand on her arm, distracting her
from the superintendent's odd behavior. "You can't
leave. You must have some quiche."

It was close to ten o'clock. The items of her to-do
list came to mind. She eyed their expectant faces
and caved. "Well, I don't have plans per se..." She

wasn't sure if it was her imagination, but the couple appeared to slump with relief.

"Good. Now that's settled. Patrick, can you set the table?" Tanya asked.

Forty minutes later, Shanna found herself sitting between two of Lynx's brothers—Brigg and Drake. The men had popped in within minutes of each other. After helping themselves to the quiche, the brothers had peppered her with questions. She didn't mind, and she found them engaging, but she never forgot that Tanya had wanted to talk. And she had been sitting at the table for two hours.

She cornered Tanya in the kitchen. Patrick was there, helping her with the dishes. "If today isn't a good day, I can—"

Before she could finish, Patrick interrupted. "No. No," he said, taking out his handkerchief to wipe his face. Shanna saw that as a sign that he was nervous. She just didn't know what was causing his nerves. "I know we set up a meeting for a couple weeks from now, but how about we go to the high school? I have some plans for renovations that I would like to discuss so we can start getting things in place this summer. We can drive together."

She bit back a groan. This meant she would have to return for her car, but she didn't want to argue since she had just gotten her job back. She looked through the kitchen window at the clear sky. Today would have been a good day to attack the weeds and trim the bushes. She traipsed behind the superintendent and sighed, knowing she wouldn't get anything accomplished outside her home today. She was so glad she had worn her sneakers. It appeared she was going to need them.

Chapter Thirty-Three

Eleven hours later, with the nonstop toiling of fifteen men plus Lynx and Hawk, Shanna's home had been transformed. Dead trees had been hewn down, shredded and their stumps removed. Weeds had been dug up, and the trees had been trimmed and now sat pretty with red mulch and white pebbles around them. They looked great against the newly painted house of pale gray and white trimming, just as Shanna had wanted. Nosy neighbors had been satisfied after Lynx declared it was a surprise for Shanna.

Once the last of the trucks had departed, Lynx and Hawk collapsed on Shanna's newly laid St. Augustine grass.

"This has got to be the craziest thing you've ever

done," Hawk huffed out. "And I'm the fool who helped you."

"I wholeheartedly agree," Lynx said. "You were a fool to help me."

They shared a laugh before giving each other a high five. Both their hands had been darkened due to the cement, and there was paint all over their shirts, but restoring the fountain had been worth it.

Lynx stood and helped his brother get to his feet. Hawk's sneakers were covered in cement, and one of them had a gash across the front. "I'll get you another pair."

"No need. I have two other ones just like them." Hawk scanned the area. "If that woman doesn't see your love through all this, she isn't worth your heart."

Lynx took out his cell phone and snapped several pictures; then he sent them to his father. Patrick called seconds later, and Lynx put the phone on speaker.

"Thank God you're done. I tried everything I could to keep her occupied, but I can tell she's ready to smother me."

"I owe you, Dad," Lynx said.

"Yes, you do. Are you boys coming by here? Your mom cooked baked chicken, mashed potatoes and green beans. She figured you'd need something to eat after all that work."

Hawk made a fist. "Yes! Kiss Mom for me. We'll be there in a few."

"Is Shanna still there?" Lynx asked.

"She left to visit her mother in the nursing home. Your mother convinced her to take some of the plum cobbler they made to give her mother."

"Mom is brilliant," Lynx said.

"Yes, you owe her big time," Patrick said.

Hawk gathered their tools and began packing them in the back of his truck. He had driven since he had all the equipment they needed to repair the fountain.

"Okay. I'll see you in a few minutes." He rushed to help Hawk get everything done. The last thing he wanted was for Shanna to pull up while he was still there.

When they departed, doubt pierced his confidence. "What if Shanna hates me for interfering?"

"Too late now," Hawk said before giving him a light punch.

Lynx covered his head with his hands. Hawk must have seen his distress because he said, "From everything you've told me, Shanna is an intelligent woman. She'll know your heart."

"Take me home," Lynx said.

"What about eating?"

"Not right now. I'll get something later."

Hawk changed directions and headed toward Lynx's house. Once they arrived, Hawk grabbed his duffel bag. "I'll spend the night with Mom and Dad. I'm hoping you'll have better company tonight."

Lynx exhaled. "Me, too, bro."

Hawk jumped into his truck and rolled down

his window. "Take my advice, little brother. If she doesn't come to you, go to her." With that, he was gone.

Chapter Thirty-Four

Shanna circled the block twice, attributing her missing her house to being bone-tired. Spending a good portion of the day with the Harringtons and then visiting her mom had sapped all her energy. At least she had made it home in time to get her UPS package. They had texted that they were four stops away. Once she had that, she would shower and get under the covers.

She slowed by her neighbor's house before her eyes went wide. Her mouth slackened, and she inched into her driveway.

She made a point to read the house number.

Yes. She was seeing right.

This was her house.

It had been painted, landscaped and the fountain...
The fountain!

Shanna turned off her car and ran across the plush lawn to hug her mother's fountain. It had been repaired—flawless—and had been painted white to match the trim of the house. Inside the fountain, a pink lotus flower floated.

Her breath caught.

Lynx.

He had done this. She was sure of it.

Shanna shook her head, amazed, speechless. Then the tears came. Her legs folded like an umbrella, and she sobbed. She was still crying when the UPS driver pulled up. She signed for the two packages, assuring the driver she was fine. She placed them behind the screen door; then she called Yanni and Laurie using FaceTime to give them a tour of the perimeter of the house.

They *ooh*ed and *aah*ed right along with her. Yanni cried when she saw their mother's fountain. Laurie loved the lotus flower.

"It symbolizes health, honor, long life and purity of heart and mind."

Shanna didn't ask how her friend knew that.

"I think I'm in love," Yanni said with a dreamy expression. "The house looks amazing. I need a man like Lynx."

"Good luck finding him." Shanna chuckled at her sister's dramatic declaration. She walked around the yard in a haze, absorbing the magnitude of work Lynx had accomplished. His family must have been in on the plan, distracting her so he could surprise her. Her heart cracked open.

"That man loves you," Laurie said, waving her arms. "He's the one. He's the one."

She nodded. "I believe you."

"He must have spent a fortune to get this done in one day," Yanni said. "'Cause that yard was worse than a hot mess."

Yeah, he must have. She froze, then gasped. He had. She placed a hand over her mouth. She wondered if Lynx had used the money he had saved to buy his grandfather's watch to fix her yard. If he had, he had used a good chunk of it. Her final doubts about Lynx disintegrated at his selfless act.

"Get off the phone and get over there," Laurie advised and gave her a wink. "He has another garden to tend."

Yanni told Shanna to wear her sexiest lingerie. Her departing words before Shanna ended the call were, "If you don't marry that man, I will."

Shanna grabbed one of the packages on her way inside. She showered, making sure to trim her "garden"; then she dressed in a pair of stilettos and a bodycon dress, wearing nothing underneath. She spritzed her body in strategic places with the Bombshell scent he liked. She hadn't been able to wear that perfume since she last saw him.

Twenty minutes later, after taming her hair, Shanna was on her way to Lynx's home, the other package in hand. She had left her purse in the car and placed the box next to it. Her heart raced, and her hands were so slippery, she had to grip the wheel all the way there. She practiced what she could say once she arrived, but nothing seemed right.

Using the spare key she had never returned, Shanna opened his front door. She had to tuck the package between her legs and hold on to her shaky hand to prevent the key from falling to the ground.

Shanna stepped into darkness and frowned. She thought Lynx would be here, waiting for her arrival. His car was outside, so she assumed he was home. She made her way to his bedroom, hearing him before she saw him. His snores were loud and long. Chuckling, she placed the package and her purse by the edge of the bed and crept under the covers beside him. He must have been really exhausted because he didn't stir once.

Lynx snuggled her close and continued sleeping.

She smiled. Even in his sleep, he wanted her. Soon, she drifted off to sleep…

Only to be awakened to Lynx's mouth on her. He behaved like a man who had discovered water after wandering in the wilderness for days. Her body heated and her release came fast and lasted long.

"Tell me I'm not dreaming," he said, cupping her face.

"You're not. I…used…my…key," she huffed out, panting between each word.

"*Mmm.* I love how ready you are for me." She heard the crinkle of a condom wrapper, and within seconds, he was loving on her. Again. "You…feel… so…good," he growled, moments before he came.

Once they had both calmed, Lynx turned on the lamp. He caressed her cheek. "I can't believe you're here with me." He gave her a light pinch on her elbow.

"Ouch." She rubbed the spot.

"Sorry, had to be sure you were real."

"I'm very real. I had to come to thank you in person." Her eyes filled. "I can't believe what you did for me. My yard is immaculate."

"I did it because I love you," he said, intertwining his leg with hers. "I needed you to see how much."

Her heart fed on his words, though his gesture had surpassed any words he could have said. She smiled at him as the tears fell. "I love you too. My mother's fountain looks brand-new." She cocked her head. "Is it?"

"No. Hawk is a sculptor. He walked me through how to mend the cracks step-by-step. It required meticulous attention and patience I didn't know I possessed, but I had to get it done."

She ran her hands through his dark strands. "I love the lotus. It added the extra touch to perfection."

His face shone; his blue eyes were earnest. "You're my lotus. You're like the whipped cream on top of pudding. Having you out of my life has been torturous. I found myself wanting to call you, to tell you even the most mundane details."

"I missed you something fierce. I knew when I woke up this morning that last night was going to be my last night without you. If you hadn't done anything, I was still coming here tonight."

His eyes widened. "What? Really?"

She nodded. "Yes. I let jealousy blind me from seeing the truth. You're a man of honor. There's no way you would sleep with two women at the same time. Deep down, I knew that. I'm sorry for misjudging you." Shanna slipped out of bed and retrieved the package; then she handed it to Lynx.

"What is it?" he asked, eyeing the box like it was a foreign object.

"Open it."

He opened the box. The only thing visible were foam peanuts. He shook his head. "Is this a gag, or does this represent something metaphorical?"

"No, silly. Look around." She chuckled. "What could be metaphorical about foam peanuts?"

"I don't know." He shrugged and felt around the box before pulling out a small box. "Is this what I think it is?" he asked with quiet reverence. His voice held such hope that tears came to her eyes.

She reached into her bag for her cell phone and recorded him opening the box. She observed his face when he held his grandfather's watch for the first time. After decades upon decades, it was finally back in the family. He swallowed back tears. "How did you afford this?"

"I didn't," she said, pressing End and walking up to him. "I wrote the new owner a letter telling him about the watch and its history, and I asked the auctioneer to forward it to him. Turns out, Mr. Winters is a true romantic. He contacted me and offered to mail the watch in exchange for another one from your collection."

Lynx nodded. "He can have them all. I have everything I need."

She smiled. "So do I."

Lynx scooped her up in his arms, "I hope you know I don't believe in long engagements."

Shanna thought of the other package—the one with her wedding dress—and smiled. "Neither do I."

* * * * *

Don't miss the next book in Michelle Lindo-Rice's Seven Brides for Seven Brothers miniseries,

Cinderella's Last Stand,

coming September 2022 from Harlequin Special Edition!

#2923 THE OTHER HOLLISTER MAN
Men of the West • by Stella Bagwell

Rancher Jack Hollister travels to Arizona to discover if the family on Three Rivers Ranch might possibly be a long-lost relation. He isn't looking for love—until he sees Vanessa Richardson.

#2924 IN THE RING WITH THE MAVERICK
Montana Mavericks: Brothers & Broncos • by Kathy Douglass

Two rodeo riders—cowboy Jack Burris and rodeo queen Audrey Hawkins—compete for the same prize all the while battling their feelings for each other. Sparks fly as they discover that the best prize is the love that grows between them.

#2925 LESSONS IN FATHERHOOD
Home to Oak Hollow • by Makenna Lee

When Nicholas Weller finds a baby in his art gallery, he's shocked to find out the baby is his. Emma Blake agrees to teach this confirmed bachelor how to be a father, but after the loss of her husband and child, can she learn to love again?

#2926 IT STARTED WITH A PUPPY
Furever Yours • by Christy Jeffries

Shy and unobtrusive Elise Mackenzie is finally living life under her own control, while charming and successful Harris Vega has never met a fixer-upper house he couldn't remodel. Elise is finally coming into her own but does Harris see her as just another project—or is there something more between them?

#2927 BE CAREFUL WHAT YOU WISH FOR
Lucky Stars • by Elizabeth Bevarly

When Chance wished for a million dollars as a teenager, he never expected it to come true—especially not via his late brother's twins, who are now his responsibility. Luckily, Poppy Digby has known the twins all their lives and agrees to stay—just for a few days!—but they each find themselves longing for more time...

#2928 EXPECTING HER EX'S BABY
Sutton's Place • by Shannon Stacey

Lane Thompson and Evie Sutton were married once and that didn't work out. But resisting each other hasn't worked out very well, either, and now they're having a baby. Can they make it work this time around? Or will old wounds once again tear them apart?

HSECNM0622

"He cannot be serious." Tansy stared at the front page of the local *Hill Country Gazette* in horror. At the far too flattering picture of Dane Knudson. And that smile. That smug, "That's right, I'm superhot and I know it" smile that set her teeth on edge. "What is he thinking?"

"He who?" Tansy's sister, Astrid, sat across the kitchen table with Beeswax, their massive orange cat, occupying her lap.

"Dane." Tansy wiggled the newspaper. "Who else?"

"What did he do now?" Aunt Camellia asked.

"This." Tansy shook the newspaper again. "'While continuing to produce their award-winning clover honey,'" she read, "'Viking Honey will be expanding operations and combining their Viking ancestry and Texas heritage—'"

Aunt Camellia joined them at the table. "All the Viking this and Viking that. That boy is pure Texan."

"The Viking thing is a marketing gimmick," Tansy agreed.

"A smart one." Astrid winced at the glare Tansy shot her way. "What about this has you so worked up, Tansy?"

"I hadn't gotten there, yet." Tansy held up one finger as she continued, "'Combining their Viking ancestry and Texas heritage for a one-of-a-kind event venue and riverfront cabins ready for nature-loving guests by next fall.'"

All at once, the room froze. *Finally.* She watched as, one by one, they realized why this was a bad thing.

Two years of scorching heat and drought had left Honey Hill Farms' apiaries in a precarious position. Not just the bees—the family farm itself.

"It's almost as if he doesn't understand or…or care about the bees." Astrid looked sincerely crestfallen.

"He *doesn't* care about the bees." Tansy nodded. "If he did, this wouldn't be happening." She scanned the paper again—but not the photo. His smile only added insult to injury.

To Dane, life was a game and toying with people's emotions was all part of it. Over and over again, she'd invested time and energy and hours of hard work, and he'd just sort of winged it. *Always.* As far as Tansy knew, he'd never suffered any consequences for his lackluster efforts. No, the great Dane Knudson could charm his way through pretty much any situation. But what would he know about hard work or facing consequences when his family made a good portion of their income off a stolen Hill Honey recipe?

Don't miss
The Sweetest Thing *by Sasha Summers,*
available June 2022 wherever
HQN books and ebooks are sold.

Harlequin.com

Get 4 FREE REWARDS!

We'll send you 2 FREE Books plus <u>plus</u> 2 FREE Mystery Gifts.

FREE
Value Over
$20

Both the **Harlequin® Special Edition** and **Harlequin® Heartwarming™** series feature compelling novels filled with stories of love and strength where the bonds of friendship, family and community unite.

*When Chance Foley wished for a million dollars as a
teenager, he never expected it to come true—especially
not via his late brother's twins, who are now his
responsibility. Luckily, Poppy Digby has known the twins
all their lives and agrees to stay—just for a few days!—
but they each find themselves longing for more time…*

Read on for a sneak peek at
Be Careful What You Wish For,
the first book in New York Times *bestselling author
Elizabeth Bevarly's new Lucky Stars miniseries!*

"Wait, what?" he interrupted again. "Logan worked for a
tech firm?"

Although his brother had taught himself to code when he
was still in middle school, and he'd been a good hacker of
the dirty tricks variety when they were teenagers, Chance
couldn't see him ever living the cubicle lifestyle for a steady
paycheck.

"Yes," Poppy said. "And he developed a computer program
several years ago that allowed companies to legally plunder
and sell all kinds of personal information and online habits of
anyone who used their websites. It goes without saying that it
was worth a gold mine to corporate America. And corporate
America paid your brother a gold mine for it."

Okay, that did actually sound like something Logan would
have been able to do. Chance probably shouldn't be surprised
that his brother would turn his gift for hacking into making a
pile of money.

Poppy pulled another piece of paper from the collection in front of her. "I have another statement that's been prepared for your trust, Mr. Foley."

He started to correct Poppy's "Mr. Foley" again, but the other part of her statement sank in too quickly. "What do you mean my trust?"

"I mean your brother and sister-in-law have put funds into a trust for you, as well."

He didn't know what to say. So he said nothing, only gazed back at Poppy, confused as hell.

When he said nothing, she continued. "The children's trust will begin to gradually revert to them when they reach the age of twenty-two. That's when the funds in your trust will revert entirely to you."

Out of nowhere, a thought popped up in the back of Chance's brain, and he was reminded of something he hadn't thought about for a long time—a wish he'd made to a comet when he was fifteen years old. A wish, legend said, that should be coming true about now, since Endicott had been celebrating the "Welcome Back, Bob" comet festival for a few weeks. Something cool and unpleasant wedged into his throat at the memory.

He eyed Poppy warily. "H-how much money is in that trust?"

Her serious green eyes had never looked more serious. "A million dollars, Mr. Foley. Once the children have reached the age of twenty-two, that million dollars will be yours."

Don't miss
Be Careful What You Wish For *by Elizabeth Bevarly,*
available August 2022 wherever
Harlequin Special Edition books and ebooks are sold.

Harlequin.com

 **HARLEQUIN**

Heartfelt or thrilling, passionate or uplifting—Harlequin is more than just happily-ever-after.

With twelve different series to choose from and new books available every month, you are sure to find stories that will move you, uplift you, inspire and delight you.

SIGN UP FOR THE HARLEQUIN NEWSLETTER

Be the first to hear about great new reads and exciting offers!

Harlequin.com/newsletters